PRAISE FOR <u>TAINTED MOONLIGHT</u>

REVIEWS FROM READERS VIA AMAZON.COM

"Loved this book from beginning to end! Erin Kelly sure knows how to draw you in and keep you turning the pages. I can't wait for the next book to be released so I can continue Korban and Sophie's story!"
– *Pamela Daniell, Author of The <u>Revelations</u> Series*

"You think you're here just to read one book? Wrong... You will be in it for the long haul. The author paints a world and characters that keep you invested in them... Love it! Can't wait for the next book to come out!"
– *Rebecca Tapia, BeccaNotBecky on YouTube*

"The book pulls you in and you don't want to put it down. Unique human and social elements seamlessly and artfully added to a great werewolf story... I was not interested in reading a werewolf story, now I cannot wait for more of the series..." – *Sylvia B.*

"If you like the *Twilight* series, you will not be disappointed. If you are a werewolf newbie such as myself, this book is a great way to break into the genre." – *David Manzano*

"A great read, looking forward to reading more from Erin Kelly!" – *L. Bilby*

"I regret waiting so long to pick up this book. Once I did I couldn't put it down... Can't wait to pick up the next in this series." – *Bluedaisy*

"I bought this at a psychic fair as I really like supporting local artists and I really can't wait for the next book. It was an easy read but with great twists and I really enjoyed it." – *Darlene A. Morehouse*

"Good book... loved that it was set in my home town! Interesting how the real world would deal with werewolves... good read." – *Jhymner*

"Clever, imaginative story that leaps off the page from the first to the last. Can't wait to see what the next "moon" brings!" – *Eileen Haynes*

WANT YOUR REVIEW IN THE NEXT BOOK?

RATE AND REVIEW <u>TAINTED MOONLIGHT</u> ON AMAZON.COM

Your feedback matters and may be published in the next story!

BOOKS BY ERIN KELLY

TAINTED MOONLIGHT

CAPTURED MOONLIGHT

INFECTED MOONLIGHT

AWAKENED MOONLIGHT*

*COMING SOON

CAPTURED MOONLIGHT

ERIN KELLY

To Jennifer –
Keep on hauling!

... Erin Kelly

ISBN: 1984285440
ISBN-13: 978-1984285447

DEDICATION

For Mom and Dad, my first fans and life-long supporters.

Thank you for all you do. I love you.

CONTENTS

1: WOLVEN IN THE WOODS

She moved like a ghost across the land, silent and swift. Even when she disturbed the branches or rustled past the long grass or leaves, any prey before her was too slow to react. There was no escape, only death for anything the golden-furred wolf encountered in her path.

Except for him of course, the great gray wolf who continued to flank her side. He was just as fast, just as strong. He was always there, always watching, but she was fine with that as long as he kept her pace.

The moon had risen and set many times, shrinking in the sky above until it was barely a thread of light. Time had no meaning here. There was only the hunt, finding water, and seeking shelter. Often she found these with her keen senses, though as the moon waned she noticed things, like how the air here was so clean, so untainted. Humans had not ventured here for decades, maybe longer. Only his musky male scent was familiar to her in this deep forest.

Ahead of them grazed a white-tailed doe, which made her salivate, until the deer lifted her head and bleated out to the nearby bushes. From the brush a tiny speckled fawn emerged and pranced over to his mother's side. This gave her pause, as there was something oddly familiar about it. The male wolf trotted over to her side and he bowed his head to sniff her. His warm, wet nose prodded her furry collar and she nipped playfully at him, before she chased him away and altered their course.

Deeper into the woods they ran, almost as one. They glided easily on four paws through grassy plains and overgrown fields; rushed past untouched forest thick with trees and splashed over tiny creeks and rushing rivers. They climbed mountains and traversed over rocks and snow that the warm spring hadn't melted away, even with summer drawing nearer with every day that passed.

She was happy here with him. She could run forever. She was finally free.

A low rumble of thunder drew her attention once more to the sky. Thick, gray clouds gathered. She knew it would rain, because she could smell it in the air hours before. She sniffed and sorted out the scents around them, and then led the way to dry ground. He remained at her side; they were two massive wolves moving together and heading towards cover as fat drops of water began to fall. She found a thick bush and crawled under it, the large leaves and tangle of branches providing shelter. He crawled in after her as the rain began to pour down around them.

She curled next to him and they settled in together. Somewhere inside her this was all still strange, but she buried those thoughts as she rested her head upon his. This was life as she knew it now. This was her normal. He soon fell asleep, though she lay awake for a long time before joining him. An opening in the sky revealed just a sliver of glowing moonlight amongst the stars right before she finally closed her eyes to rest.

2: WILDERNESS

She woke to a duality of sensations, his warm, solid body curled in front of her as she pressed her cheek against his smooth shoulder; behind her was the cool, damp grass. Groggy, she opened her eyes and rubbed them sleepily. It took only a second for her to register that she'd done this with her hand.

She stared at her hand for a long moment, marveled at it even. Every joint and muscle in her body seemed to ache, but she was back to normal. She wiggled her fingers, her toes. No doubt about it she was definitely human again.

Curled in fetal position as he slept alongside her, Korban had also returned to his two-legged state. She ran her fingers through his hair and smoothed down the dark strands. How had they gotten here? Where exactly was here? Then the very human question popped into her mind— where could she find some clothes?

She shivered from the chill in the air and curled closer to Korban as she tried to remember how they'd ended up here. The forest that surrounded them was dense, a lush green even in the darkness. The thick scent of pine and the sweet scent of maple tickled her nose, and she resisted a sneeze. That fresh, lovely perfume that came with the fresh rain was everywhere. The flora was accompanied by the musk of wildlife, along with their many sounds: the worms and moles that rustled in the wet earth below them, the hoot of an owl nestled in the branches of a nearby tree, and Korban's steady heartbeat, echoed by his light snoring.

There were no other signs or smells of any human beings here, and a knot loosened in her stomach. She couldn't hurt anyone out here.

Hurt… the thought triggered her memory with a sudden jolt. Images flashed before her eyes. Her eyes moved to where the needle had struck her, and as if it had hit her again, she could feel the sudden strike of metal piercing her, the burning of the dark serum as it coursed through her veins. Nikki's cruel words, her cold tone. Matt aiming the gun, the click when he pulled the trigger.

She cried out and Korban stirred. She muffled her whimper by biting the back of her hand, and tried not to wake him just yet.

Nikki had forced her to turn, to be rid of her once and for all. Now here they were, in a forest – who knows where – and she'd spent a countless number of days – weeks, maybe months – as a wolf.

Her memories as a wolf were hazy, more feelings and scents than pictures. Though from her scent lingering with Korban's, it was obvious he had remained by her side the entire time. Just as he had the whole time she'd known him, since the fateful night she had been attacked and infected. Her own sister had orchestrated all of it.

Clothes. Need clothes, and shelter.

She shoved the memories back as quickly as they resurfaced. She had to focus on finding out where they ended up, getting clothes, shelter, food and water, and finding out how much time had passed. Then… then she could think about all the rest.

As much as it would be a creature comfort to have clothes, she was certain there wasn't a Macy's or even a Walmart nearby, so perhaps seeking shelter should take priority. Maybe then they could somehow get their bearings and locate some clues as to where on earth they had ended up.

Sophie gazed up to the sky again, toward the fading stars as the sun began to rise. She let Korban rest more for now and watched for a moment as he dreamed, blissfully unaware of the situation they now found themselves in. Soon enough he would wake up and realize their predicament, but perhaps by then she could at least have an answer to one of their problems. Slowly and quietly she moved away from the warmth of his body, and the cool night air caused goosebumps to spread over her skin. The damp leaves seemed even colder as she crawled from the safety of their shallow den beneath the overgrown shrub, the morning dew and remnants of rain drops like ice on her bare skin. Korban shuddered, and for a moment it seemed he would wake up, but she watched as he curled into himself then murmured under his breath as he resumed his sleep.

Standing up felt strange after running on four legs for so long. Her first few steps felt unsure, and she used the trunk of a nearby oak tree to steady herself.

The sky was slowly growing lighter as she began her bare foot trek through the woods. The ground here was still soft and damp from the rain but she already missed the ease of traveling on four paws. Human feet felt awkward and weird as she explored the surrounding area. The dense foliage at least seemed to cover her nakedness as she scanned around them.

Trees, tall grass, and then a bush with familiar, ripe, red berries clumped on it – raspberries – came into view. She plucked one and sniffed it to be sure, rolling it in between her fingers. After weeks of a diet that consisted predominantly of raw meat, her stomach churned a little in memory, and the first sweet bite of raspberry was divine.

She devoured a couple dozen before she slowed down and listened as the world around her began to wake. She strained her ears, but the only human-like sounds for miles came from her and Korban's light snoring under the bush nearby.

A creature burrowed through the damp earth while a small herd of deer grazed in a nearby clearing. Squirrels chittered and chased one another around a maple tree. A mosquito buzzed by but thankfully seemed to ignore her. The wind rustled leaves far from where she stood, and a moment later, she felt it blow past her. No scent or faint sound of cars traveling past were to be found, nor the steady hum of electricity to interfere out here.

She ate another handful or so of the raspberries before she began to collect some for Korban. They would need water, but she could hear a steady stream nearby and was certain as untouched as this area was the water would be okay to drink. She spied a large leaf – an elephant ear – she recalled its name from an early memory of camping long ago. She snapped one off and used it as a make-shift bowl to collect a bunch more berries. She contemplated the other uses of the large leaves. Maybe there was a way to weave them together with the long grass to form some sort of covering until they located clothes.

She gathered up some more leaves and long stalks of grass, and then returned to the temporary den where Korban still rested. She settled back under the bush beside him, careful not to spill the raspberries into the dirt, and began to braid the long grass together. She made a decent length of rope by the time he stirred again, and this time his brilliant golden eyes opened. "Sophie... you're back!" His smile was contagious, and she laughed as his brow knitted in realization. "I'm back too."

"So I noticed." She knotted the length of grass together and wrapped it around her waist. Her smile sobered. "I'm not sure where we ended up, but it seems that toxin wasn't as permanent as we were led to believe."

"Wow," Korban said, and gazed at his hands in wonder as he flexed his fingers. "I guess that's lucky for us... at least that we're human again anyway. I wonder what changed us back."

"Maybe the serum is out of our systems now." Sophie shrugged, and then carefully poked a hole into one of the elephant ears before she strung the grass rope through it. It tore easily, which was good and bad. Temporary clothes were better than nothing, however, so she set about stringing more together until she had herself a skirt. "I brought you some raspberries I found."

His eyes shone with gratitude. "Thanks." He scooped up the leaf and popped a red berry in his mouth. He polished off most of them and she glanced his way as she worked on weaving the grass into a loose, leafy top. He averted his own gaze respectfully, but also seemed deep in thought. "We have to find out where we are... and we have to get back to Syracuse."

She knew this was true, hell she had thought about it herself. Yet as the memories begin to resurface, a new fear coursed through her at the thought of returning home. Clearly the idea disturbed Korban just as much, because the expression of dread was more than apparent on his face too. His gaze softened as he tried to reassure her. "One thing at a time for now. Though it looks like you covered breakfast and our clothes."

She smirked and nodded, then handed him one of her grass-woven ropes. "See if this will wrap around you. It's not much but at least if we do stumble upon a forest ranger or campers they won't freak out... as much."

He accepted the rope and wrapped it around his hips. Her estimated length was correct. He grinned at her, with that mischievous light returning to his eyes. "Think next time you can make something with a fig leaf? It's so much more slimming."

Sophie cracked a smile at that remark. She finished adding leaves to her top, which was more a necklace than a halter-top, but it would provide some modest coverage at least. She joked as she tied the coverlet in place over her chest, "I suppose right now it does feel like we are the only two people in existence. A werewolf version of Adam and Eve."

Korban chuckled at that, then finished the raspberries and looked around, nostrils flaring as he took in their surroundings. After a moment he frowned. "Looks like we have a long walk in store, no matter what direction we go in."

Sophie nodded and looked up to the sky. "The sun is rising from the east, unless that has changed while we were wolves. We can head north, but what if we accidentally cross over into Canada... if we haven't already done that."

Korban bobbed his head in agreement. "That may cause more problems than solve them. Crossing the border without permission in general is frowned upon, never mind as a werewolf."

"So we'll head south then and hope we don't end up somewhere in Pennsylvania," Sophie said, then stood, her grass skirt rustling as she moved. "Maybe we'll find some actual clothing on the way."

Korban nodded and crawled out of their temporary den, stretching and moving slowly as he readjusted to walking upright again. "Maybe we should get some more of those raspberries for the road and some water. If we stick close to the streams we won't have to worry about finding something to carry it in."

As much as she dreaded returning home, she was glad when they began to move, each carrying as many leaf-wrapped raspberries as they could hold. They followed near the bank of a steady stream that smelled clean and kept their eyes and ears open, noses constantly seeking out signs of civilization. The air began to warm as the sun rose higher into the sky, but the shady forest kept them cool as they walked along. She shivered; the make-shift clothes provided no real warmth against the shadows of the forest. Korban took her hand; his was warm and comforting. She smiled to him and squeezed his hand as they walked along in a comfortable silence. She wasn't sure how she would have managed any of this without him.

Even lost and naked in the woods she felt so grateful to have him by her side.

3: JOURNEY

They walked together in silence for a while, keeping quiet to listen to the world around them. The forest was full of new sounds and scents that were delightful to their senses. Korban kept her hand in his, and while they wandered alongside the bank of the stream, he smiled. "Pops used to take us fishing during the summer," he remembered. "Alex's grandfather loved working with cars and machines, but he also loved nature. He wanted to make sure we knew how to do certain things like build a fire or clean a fish. We would go camping, and fishing and he would make it special."

After a moment she smiled too, and added, "We would go on a big family trip every summer. One of my favorite trips was a camping one. My father had this great idea… and everything you can imagine that could go wrong, did go wrong. He had no idea how to build our tent or how to fish, but he tried based on what he'd seen in movies and on TV. Even when we tried to swim in the lake, we got leeches on us and Nikki screamed like she was—" Sophie started to laugh, but stopped short and shook her head, gazing down with a solemn version of her smile.

He wasn't sure what to say or how to comfort her. He'd never felt that deep of a betrayal. He gently squeezed her hand and they continued along in silence for another few minutes.

Sophie sighed and changed the subject, "What I wouldn't give for a hot bath right now, or just a clean pair of my own underwear."

Korban nodded and stepped over a fallen tree branch that was half submerged in the babbling brook. "Or a cup of coffee," he added. The path before them suddenly opened up and he stopped, eyes widening. "Whoa…"

Their path ended and exposed a lush, green valley that spread for miles. The leafy, emerald green was only broken up by a handful of large bodies of water that stretched out and reflected the clear blue sky. From where they stood he couldn't see any buildings or houses. They truly had ended up far out in the wilderness. Not even a tell-tale trail of smoke wafted up from a camp site to guide them back to civilization. Only the wild mountains could be seen for miles.

~*~

Later that night, after they covered countless miles and found shelter under an old, massive, oak tree, Korban was happy to sit on the pile of leaves they had gathered. He was even more content when Sophie curled close to him for warmth. The night wasn't that chilly, but he certainly wasn't going to complain at her desire to be close to him.

She rested her head on his shoulder with a soft sigh. "It's so peaceful out here… but noisy at the same time."

He gently laughed at this, understanding her meaning. The creatures of the night were awakening now, replacing the song of the day with the music of the night. Her hair fell softly against his skin. Something about the simple action made him feel a deep contentment as her warm skin pressed against his own.

She shivered and he wrapped his arms around her, not even

thinking of his own chilliness, though holding her close combated the night air for both of them. He shouldn't feel this at ease out in the wilderness, naked and lost in the forest, but the subdued wolf that lingered inside felt at home here. Especially with her by his side.

A small fire crackled before them, a combined effort from skills Pops had taught him long ago and Sophie's training as a girl scout. When he'd inquired if she had earned a fuzzy badge for camping out as a werewolf, she cracked a smile, but didn't say much else about it. More than likely it brought up memories of her sister, and he was wise enough to not press the issue.

He had sensed Nikki's coldness the first time he had met her, but even then he had no idea what kind of monster they had been dealing with. Nikki's true colors had been revealed in the worst way, and no doubt Sophie was still reeling from it all. Korban couldn't believe it himself, and to him Nikki Winters was a stranger. Sophie was horrifically betrayed by her sister, someone she loved and trusted. Nikki did worse than stab her own sister in the back. Somehow she had dispatched a Wolven on her in a cruel attempt to brutally murder Sophie, and instead damned her to become a werewolf.

When Sophie not only survived the attack but her first transformation as well, Nikki used Sophie's love for her son to lure her out of hiding and bombed their home, nearly killing his best friend and roommate Alex.

Alex. RJ.

His two roommates – friends – no, his brothers. His family. A deep longing burrowed in his gut as he worried about them. Was RJ being held responsible for his running away? Was he in jail because as a sponsor he was being punished in Korban's place? Was Alex recovering from his broken arm, burns, and the smoke inhalation from the explosion?

They had to get back home. If only there was some way to find out where they'd ended up, or if they found shelter, maybe there would be some clues. Or better yet, run into someone who could tell them. Of course there would be an initial awkwardness, given the fact that right now their Adam and Eve cosplay would certainly raise eyebrows.

For now there was nothing he could do for RJ or Alex, except to find their way back home to them. Protecting Sophie and finding shelter, clothes, and food were his top priorities. He would return home and set things right again but in the meantime he had to trust that his words to Officer McKinnon were enough to keep his roommate out of too much trouble.

4: DISCOVERY

Their luck would turn that following day as they journeyed deeper into the forest. They had traveled most of that morning and continued through midday when the trees thinned out and they came upon a small clearing along a narrow path leading from the river.

Nestled in long, uncut grass was an older style camper. A long, silver-colored Streamline speckled with spots of rust. After days without running into any sign of human life, it was startling to stumble upon this big of a find. Eyes widening, Sophie glanced around and tensed. If they ran into others, would she be strong enough not to attack them, as she had Alex before?

A second glance revealed she might not have to worry so much, rather, her first wary sniff of the air uncovered no trace of another human's scent. Whoever managed to get this camper so far into the forest had abandoned it a while ago.

Korban flashed her a grin and the knot in her stomach loosened. "Looks like it's our lucky day," he said, then carefully waded through the long, thick grass toward the camper.

An eerie stillness seemed to linger in the area as they approached the metallic door. The hinges were speckled with red and brown rust but appeared to be still in good condition otherwise. "Camping season may have just started, I think," Korban said softly and tilted his head to listen again inside.

She strained to hear as well but the camper was definitely empty. Korban reached for the door and knocked anyway, just in case, and the sound seemed to echo like a drum in the silence around them. No sound followed, and no answer came from within. "If there is someone who owns this nearby… maybe it is better to ask forgiveness than permission in our case."

She nodded. It wasn't like they had too many options, so she didn't protest when he tried for the door. To both their surprise, the door opened without hesitation. Korban exchanged a glance with her, gave a nervous smile, and said, "Our luck really is turning for the better. I was sure I would have to pick the lock to break in or something."

"I suppose if the owner comes and finds us here that may work in our favor towards forgiveness," Sophie smiled in return. "Just entering their camper, instead of breaking in first."

He grinned at this, and then opened the door wider. "Let's see if they left any clues as to where we are."

She followed him inside the dark camper, uncertain what to expect. The rounded windows all had the blinds drawn, but it took only a few seconds for her keen eyes to adjust to the darkness. Inside the camper was cramped but clean. Almost too clean at first glance, with barely a speck of dust along the counters that lined a tiny kitchen. Immediately next to it was a couch with a small, pull-out table, along with the front end of the camper. A beaded curtain divided the kitchen from a narrow hall where two thin, long beds were neatly made, not even a wrinkle to the pristine bed sheets. Further in the back was a tiny bathroom, with a toilet, sink, and narrow shower stall. A small closet held an empty suitcase and a pressed suit hanging in a garment bag. The little drawers, built into the camper beneath the bed, held rows of neatly rolled shirts, pants, socks, and men's underwear.

Korban ran a hand along the flat, seamless blanket tucked neatly over the bed. "It's like whoever stayed here was militaristic in their cleaning and orderliness."

Sophie nodded and opened one of the built-in cabinets in the kitchen. An assortment of canned goods were arranged just as orderly as the man's underwear, but she could appreciate the bounty of food that was more substantial than raspberries. She took a can out of the cupboard to examine the expiration date, which wasn't for another couple of years yet, if her calculations were still correct. She frowned thoughtfully and wondered out loud, "Do you know... or have any idea on how much time we lost?"

Korban emerged from behind the beaded curtain wearing a faded pair of jeans and a white t-shirt, both which seemed a little loose on him. "I... that is a really good question," he said, scratching the back of his head. "I was wondering that too. It has to have been a couple weeks at least. I was aware of time as a wolf, but my wolf didn't seem to care about it as much as I did."

"Maybe there is something in here that will give us a clue to that too," Sophie sighed, then sized him up. "Seems you found some clothes to borrow at least."

"I found some that may fit you too. Though I've personally drawn a line to not borrow another man's underwear." He grinned. "Too neatly rolled. I am sure whoever this guy is, he'd lose it if I meddled with his unmentionables. Not that I'd blame him."

Sophie laughed and shook her head. "So what did you find me to wear?"

Korban held up a small bundle of gray sweatpants and another white shirt and she was more than happy to put them on and shed away her crumbling plant ensemble. Never before had sweatpants felt so heavenly, the warm and soft material welcomed more than ever after a long day of work. "Oh, that's nice," she sighed contently, and though the material was a bit loose on her frame as well, at least the elastic band rested at her hips.

They had shelter, clothes, and food to boot. Now they could search for clues as to where their oasis was located deep in the heart of the mountains.

They searched the neat and organized kitchenette for more clues but only turned up more dry goods, such as some freeze-dried fruit and powdered milk. Korban's eyes lit up when he discovered a bag of beef jerky and he unceremoniously opened the bag. The smoky scent of meat wafted in the air and made her empty stomach growl in anticipation. He extended the bag towards her and she didn't hesitate to snatch several strips from the plastic bag. Her teeth easily shredded the slightly-stale, tough jerky in no time.

For a moment she couldn't recall the last time she had meat, and then flashes of images emerged from her memory. Running, hunting in the wild forest. Korban panting at her side. The rush of blood as she ripped into the throat of a rabbit. The heavenly chunks of fresh meat that she tore from the fallen creature.

She slowed herself down as her human side's stomach lurched at the memory. Korban leaned against the pantry door and thoughtfully nibbled on his piece of beef jerky. "Whoever owns this camper is ready for the season. Pretty organized and well stocked. We'll have to thank them and eventually replace what we use. Not like we really have much of a choice at this point. I hope they'll understand."

"Knowing our luck we'll get a shoot-first-and-ask-questions-later camper instead of a happy one," Sophie said and smirked to him, and then polished off another piece of dried meat.

"Hopefully we'll find out where we are so we can get back home before that happens," Korban said, and Sophie tensed. His smile faded and a look of concern took its place. "You don't want to go back to Syracuse?"

There was no hiding it from him. Not that she wanted to hide anything from him. "I… I'm not sure that I'm ready to go home yet," Sophie sighed. "If we do find out where we are I would like to maybe take a day before we head back. Or two."

Korban gave her a sympathetic look and nodded. "I suppose we could both use it. I'm not sure what will happen when we do get back. They may put us in… well, it's better we enjoy the fresh air while we can. I just… I need to go back, or they'll lock RJ up. If they haven't already."

Sophie nodded, the icy feeling still rooted in her stomach. "Of course. We will go back, together. I just… I need a little time to digest what happened."

Nikki and Lucas. Nikki's betrayal. Her memory dredged up vivid parts, her sister's cruel confession playing on repeat in her head. She looked away from Korban and slowly chewed on another strip of jerky. It was strange how she felt safer here with Korban, wearing a stranger's clothes and snacking on stolen jerky, than she felt even thinking about returning home.

She closed her eyes and shuddered, and his arms tentatively wrapped around her. She turned and buried her face into the warm, tan skin of his neck and inhaled his scent.

She'd held in so much while they struggled to survive in the wilderness, but now that they were here her walls began to crumble down. Her arms slid around him; she just held onto him tight and breathed. His lips brushed her ear when he softly whispered, "I'm here with you."

So many clichés ran through her mind; that he was her rock, the port during a storm. Her pillar and strength when her knees were weak. All true in this moment. She clung on to him a little tighter, but didn't collapse into a fit of sobs. She simply breathed in his masculine scent, a potpourri of forest and wolf, and tightly held on to him for a long time.

5: SHELTER

It was strange to sleep indoors after having an open sky above them for so long, yet as the rain began to pelt the tin roof he was grateful for the shelter. Though there were two beds available, Sophie laid curled against him, and the pair crowded together on one of the narrow bunks. Her breathing had evened out after some time had passed and he knew she was asleep. Even as comfortable as he was, his mind was racing, and keeping him awake. Even cramped together on a flat mattress, he was content. He was sure he could bear any conditions as long as Sophie was with him, especially after they had survived in the wilderness together. *Survivor, Naked and Afraid*— hell, they'd done it without the comfort of camera crews. No safety net to rely on, only each other, and that was enough.

He watched the drops of water as they streaked across the window pane, and thunder rumbled and boomed in the distance. A warning for the storm that was to come. His mind drifted back to thoughts of RJ and Alex. They did need to return home, yet he could understand Sophie's hesitation. His own stomach churned in worry at what awaited their return.

Sophie's fingers curled against his chest and she softly murmured, "Can't sleep either?"

He smiled. She never ceased to surprise him. "It's strange having a roof over our heads," and he gazed up to it, the constant pinging of rain against the metal like a steady beat.

"Yeah," she agreed, and they laid there listening to the rhythm of the rain on the roof for a long, peaceful moment. She looked up to him, and his eyes moved from the ceiling to her. "I was thinking… how it's strange that I trust you more than anyone else in this world, but I know so little about you." She gave him a smile. "Not that you haven't earned that trust."

He nodded and simply said, "All right. I'm an open book. Ask me anything. I'm more than happy to share."

She took a moment, looking pensive as a gust of wind rattled the sides of the trailer. "What was your childhood like?" Sophie asked, and settled in against him to listen.

"Overall, pretty happy," Korban began, thinking back with a smile. "I grew up on the same block as Alex and RJ, up the street from the garage in an apartment with my mom. Mom worked hard and made sure I didn't go without." He paused and his smile sobered a little. "She did the same for Ace, my best friend, when his mother went missing. Everyone who knew her loved her. She held down a day job, a night job, and still found time to raise me and help others." He swallowed and took a deep breath. "When Pops lost his wife, she would bring him meals and he would keep her car running. Alex and I became good friends, and the rest is history."

"I bet the three… four of you had a lot of adventures growing up," Sophie said softly.

He chuckled and nodded. "Yeah, we got into all kinds of trouble together. Usually nothing too serious. Alex would get these ideas… sometimes he would talk the rest of us into them. Sometimes we were bored." He smirked. "We would help Pops around the garage, running errands for him or RJ's parents or Mom. We'd spend our allowance on snacks and comic books, or go to the movies once in a while. Pretty average stuff, I guess."

Her smile widened at this revelation. "I didn't realize you were a nerd."

He made a face at this and she giggled. "Hey! I find that term offensive. I prefer geek, or comic book enthusiast."

She laughed and rolled over on her stomach, propping her head up on her hands. "So you spent many nights reading comics with your friends, and days helping out at home and the garage."

"Yeah," his smile sobered again. "It was our home away from home, until it actually became my home."

He wondered if when they returned they could go back home to the garage, or if the garage would still be under repair. He couldn't fathom never being able to return to his home. The garage, Cyrus Autos, had to be salvageable. It hurt too much to even think that they could lose their home on top of everything else.

"I loved reading when I was young too," Sophie supplied with a wistful smile. "I still enjoy a good book. Even after I started law school and was reading mountains of text books on law, I couldn't resist a good crime thriller when I had the time."

"Law school huh?" Korban blinked, though he knew he shouldn't be too surprised. Sophie was incredibly intelligent. "You seem too honest to be a lawyer."

"Ha, ha." She rolled her eyes, and an amused smile broke through.

Korban amended, "I knew you were smart, but that's incredible. Did you finish?"

Sophie's smile wavered and she shook her head. "I found out I was expecting Daniel while I was studying for the bar exam. I began reading more books on motherhood instead of law. I told myself I'd go back to it again eventually, once Danny was older. I finished my classes, but didn't take the bar exam. Maybe I should have, but…" she trailed off for a moment, then smiled and shook her head. "Now more than ever I treasure being there for my son. I was so lucky to have the time I did with him. I saw his first smile, his first steps… I miss him so much." She looked away as her voice trembled. "Do you think… when we get back… maybe I could see him again?"

A lump formed in his throat as he became overwhelmed by the heartbreak rolling off her. He gently placed his hand on her shoulder and she leaned into his touch. The laws were clear about this, but they were wrong. He wasn't sure what would happen when they returned home, but he would do everything in his power to reunite Sophie with her son. "Maybe," he said softly as he clung on to hope, "if they see you're in control, not the wolf, I think it is possible."

She nodded and met his eyes, her own glistening with unshed tears. "I want to see him again. I want to hold him. I want to be able to control my wolf side, and be myself again."

"You've already come so far, Sophie, I know you'll be able to control your wolf. They'll assign you to a handler. I know someone will sponsor you, like RJ did for me." Korban lightly threaded his fingers through her golden hair to comfort her. "Things may never be the same as they were before, but it doesn't mean that it won't get better. We survived the impossible; we came back from the brink of losing our humanity. I don't think there is anything that you and I can't do together."

Sophie smiled at his words, and the devastating scent of her heartache faded away, replaced by the pleasant perfume of renewed hope and incredible gratitude. She leaned in and as their lips met the thunder rumbled. The rain continued to pour like buckets around them, but all he heard was her heartbeat echoing his own.

~*~

She woke up before he did, before the sun rose and the dark night sky remained dominant above them, quiet and speckled with twinkling stars between thin stretches of lingering clouds. Careful not to wake Korban from his slumber, she gently pulled away from the warm nest of his arms. She was restless, but that didn't mean he had to give up his sleep on her account. She tiptoed towards the door and stepped outside. The air was fresh but damp, the passing storm rinsing the old to give way to the new.

Somehow they'd made it so far, together. She sat down on the stoop and let the cool air wash over her, the after rain scent poured in to replace the stagnant, stale air inside the camper.

A tear escaped and rolled down her cheek. The memories were returning and more solid now. The way Nikki sneered at her, for surviving all her malicious schemes. Her sister's betrayal. Her husband... and her sister. The two people she loved and trusted had been having an affair. Nikki had decided she wanted Sophie out of the picture permanently. The whole idea made her sick to her stomach. Pain didn't begin to describe what she felt, the deepest heartache she'd ever experienced wracking through her.

Lucas and Nikki. Nikki and Lucas.

When they returned home she could confront Lucas about the whole ordeal. As for her sister...

Fire, smoke, blood. Tires squealing and the sound of twisting metal. Nikki...

Could she have survived such an awful wreck? Even though she had put her through hell, the thought of her sister dying like that... it made her even more heart sick.

You can't focus on that now, Sophie. She chastised herself as she stood up. She carefully closed the door, left it slightly ajar, and walked around the clearing for a moment. Moving around the yard already made her feel a tiny bit better. Their basic needs of food and shelter now taken care of, of course these feelings would find a way to come crashing through. She had to face the fact that the two people she loved most had betrayed her. How deeply involved Lucas was in her sister's scheme was still unclear, but when they returned home she was going to the police, and then...

Then she would endure the fallout, come what may.

We are survivors.

Korban's earlier words gave her some comfort even as he lightly snored in the camper. A small smile tugged the corner of her mouth, only to widen when her eyes fell upon something she'd overlooked before. A clue as to where they'd ended up in the wilderness.

So excited by this discovery, an idea bubbled up from the back of her mind and she quietly crept back into the camper. It was so simple, she felt silly for overlooking it before. Sure enough, she found another hint to their location by rummaging through a small waste basket that contained crinkled up papers in it. She was elated by the discovery but stopped herself from disturbing Korban's sleep. While the clues she had found didn't pinpoint their exact location, it at least gave them a starting point. She wouldn't wake him just yet, and instead she busied herself by preparing a breakfast for them that was more substantial than wild berries.

Sophie heated a can of corned beef hash over the charcoal grill outside. She divided the contents of the can in half, saving some for Korban, but before she took her first bite, the door to the camper opened up, and while sniffing the air he stumbled out, his dark, brown hair still disheveled from sleep.

"Sorry, I should have known the smell would wake you up, even out here," Sophie apologized, but he simply smiled and shrugged.

"Pops used to say if you ain't getting up for breakfast, then you ain't getting up for anything," he walked over and licked his lips. "That smells amazing."

Sophie smirked. "I know my way around a can opener," she said, then added as she used the spatula to serve from the frying pan, "I found some clues as to where we ended up."

"Breakfast with good news? You are continuing to impress me, as always." Korban took the plate she offered him, but seemed more eager to hear what she had to say.

She didn't keep him in suspense, instead she gestured to the camper itself. "The license plate is a bit rusted, but we're still in New York. I dug up an old grocery receipt inside just in case, but it seems we are still in our home state at least. Possibly near a small town called Haskell."

"So we made it up to the Adirondacks, I think," Korban said, glancing around in amazement. "Maybe we can hike and find a road. There must be one close by for this camper to end up here."

Sophie nodded and took a few bites before she spoke again. "What do you think may happen when we return to Syracuse, back to civilization again?"

Korban chewed thoughtfully then swallowed. "They may have us put into quarantine for a little while… for questioning, and to make sure we are stable for the outside again." She noticed how the color seemed to drain from him at this and she reached to him, put her hand over his. "I am hoping that Officer McKinnon will have our backs, and I'm sure Tim will, but even if he does that won't guarantee that we won't spend some time locked up. Tested on."

He shuddered and she squeezed his hand. The acrid scent of fear tinged his forest-like smell as painful memories resurfaced. "We'll think of something," she reassured him then squeezed his hand tighter. "We don't have to head back right this moment. Soon, but not now… maybe we could stay here until the next full moon. Have one last run together out here in the wild. Then we can go home. Together."

Korban looked uncertain, but after a moment he relaxed, looking relieved. "We haven't smelled any humans around here for miles, and it's early in the camping season, I think, so it is possible… it would be nice." He smiled. "Do you remember anything from when we were wolves?"

"Just small bits and pieces," she said, remembering fuzzy pictures like an out of focus clip show. "Better than the first time, when it was all a blank. What about you?"

"I remember a lot, but it's like… watching a movie with subtitles. I remember what I saw but I don't understand all of it, as it was from the wolf's point of view. Luckily you put the clues together and we now have some idea as to where we are." He slid his hand over hers, their fingers intertwining. "I'm lucky to be lost in the wilderness with such a smart lady."

She smiled at his compliment and they finished breakfast. One can of hash wasn't nearly enough to completely halt the wolf's hunger, but it did keep it at bay for now. Their human sensibility had to ration what they did have until they were out of the woods. "Why don't we go for a walk and see if we can find the road? We can try a new direction each day, until we find it," Sophie suggested, and he nodded in agreement.

"Good plan," he said, and took her empty plate. "Maybe we can find some fresh water again too. Somewhere we can refill our water reserves."

She nodded in agreement. He cleaned up their plates and she pulled out a couple pairs of men's sandals for them to walk in. "I wonder who he is, the man who owns these, and this camper," Sophie mused as they walked along the direction she'd picked.

"Someone very practical, thankfully." Korban glanced around, his senses on high alert. "We'll have to figure out a way to thank him somehow. Hopefully he understands the bind we are in and doesn't charge us with… well, I guess not so much breaking in, but entering his camper."

"Maybe we can replace everything we use," she said, stepping carefully over a fallen log and sniffing the air for clues, such as any hint of a road or passing vehicle. Smells of exhaust, cement, rubber, or asphalt. "I smell water this way. At least we aren't too far from a source."

Korban gave her an impressed smile. "It seems like you have a stronger sense of smell than I do."

She smirked and gave him a playful look. "I'm probably faster, too," she said, and he raised an eyebrow. She merely winked to him. "Race you there."

"Really?" he asked her, to which her grin widened.

"Last one there does dishes for the week!" Then she bolted, causing him to exclaim from behind her, "Hey!"

The two raced through the forest, until the trees gave way to a clearing that revealed a breathtaking sight: an expanse of muddy, rocky shore yielding to a clear, shimmering lake that mirrored the morning colors of the sky above. A small, wooden pier stretched from the edge of the muddy banks and went several yards out into the lake. Sophie heard Korban as he sprinted to catch up with her, and she stepped out onto the dock carefully. The wood was worn and weathered, but sturdy. She heard Korban halt as he took a sharp breath and knew he was moved by the sight as much as she was. She glanced over her shoulder at him, giving him a smug and victorious look. "I'll have time to do some fishing while you take care of the dishes."

"Not fair, I demand a rematch," Korban chuckled breathlessly and joined her out on the dock. "This is… incredible. No wonder the camper is so off the grid."

"It is the perfect get away." Sophie gazed out over the lake, which was teeming with life in its fresh water.

She stepped further out on the pier and something came over her. She looked to Korban, then pulled her shirt – rather the borrowed man's shirt – over her head, then dropped it onto the ground before removing the loaned sweatpants, letting them pool into a pile before she stepped to the edge of the dock, took a deep breath, then jumped in.

The water was freezing. She gasped as she resurfaced and goose-bumps broke out over her skin. She glanced back in time to see Korban shed away his own borrowed clothes, then do a cannonball into the lake, splashing her with a wave of cold water as he landed. He emerged, sputtering and teeth chattering. "WHOA that's c-cold!"

She laughed and gave him a playful splash, which caused him to laugh and retaliate with another splash. They spent the morning splashing and swimming together and for the first time in a long while Sophie felt truly care free.

~*~

The next few days they searched and explored in several directions, but didn't find the road that might guide them home. Each day that passed seemed a little easier, though she dreaded the morning they would find asphalt and road signs that would lead them from this wooded sanctuary and point them back home. Away from this slice of paradise that made their problems seem so far away.

Since they found the lake, fresh fish was now a part of the dinner menu. Using a fishing pole they found and proving she was no slouch, Sophie showed Korban a few tricks she knew from her summers in Girl Scouts and time on her grandfather's boat. After they hiked to seek out the road they would spend the afternoon hours out at the lake, swimming and fishing. They spent moments together in silence at times, and others were filled with laughter. They grew closer, with Korban opening up to her as she did to him. She learned so much about his past as they lay out on the dock and talked. He shared much about his history as they watched the sun crawl across a blue, endless sky.

"My mother would have really liked it here. She loved nature. She would have liked you, too. She was always hard working and told me never to settle for someone who wasn't willing to work, too." Korban's yellow eyes had a faraway look as he reminisced.

Sophie turned to him, hesitant at first, but then she gently asked, "What about your father?"

He blinked at her question, an uncomfortable look briefly crossing over him, then a hard neutral expression took over. "What about him?"

"You told me in the graveyard about how he abandoned your mother and you," Sophie said as she reached and took his hand. She could feel the tension singing from his body. "I was wondering if you had any memories of him."

He took a deep breath and kept his gaze up on the sky. At first she wondered if he had shut her out, that she crossed a line by asking this taboo topic. She opened her mouth to apologize but he said, "I guess I haven't really said much about him before. He was never really around for me, so I sort of gave up even talking about him a long time ago." He paused. "He has never really been a part of my life, so I don't bring him up."

She squeezed his hand. "That is his loss. He has no idea what an incredible son he has."

Korban scoffed at that and shook his head. She flinched at the harsh sound but he turned his gaze to her and his expression softened. "Believe me, if you knew him, you would know that he doesn't feel that way. He chose to leave my mother before I was born, and started a different family. He wasn't there when Mom was sick, or when she died. I'm not worth his time so he isn't worth mine either. That's all."

"Well... he is wrong," Sophie insisted and caressed his cheek with her hand, evoking a smile from him.

She dropped the subject and he seemed all too happy to say nothing more on it for now.

~*~

After a few days of heavy rain, enough to keep them closed up in the camper, they were both relieved when one evening it stopped. It had been bad enough that they had paused their exploration of the forest, spending their time chatting and searching the camper floor to ceiling for any more clues they had overlooked. Sophie had her head resting in his lap as she was reading a Stephen King novel when the rain slowed, then ceased. An eerie quiet filled the air in the absence of the constant percussion of raindrops pelting the roof.

Korban had been dozing off but the sudden silence sent a jolt through him. "Finally," he said softly, but it seemed loud in the quiet camper.

She smiled, lowered her book, and glanced up to him. "You've got cabin fever too, hmm?"

He felt his cheeks warm as he confessed, "Yeah… I'm not a fan of being confined in small spaces. I'm a claustrophobic werewolf."

She gently chuckled, put a playing card into her book as a bookmark, and said, "Well, we're top of the food chain around here. Why don't we take our sleeping bag outside if it's clear enough?"

"Sleeping under the stars sounds wonderful after being cooped up for so long," he said.

He got up as Sophie sat up and went to the door. Opening it and peering outside, they saw a swollen three-quarter moon glowing in the sky, with thin wisps of cloud floating here and there as the storm drifted off into the distance. They gathered up the sleeping bag, blankets, and sheets and headed outside into the fresh air.

He spread the waterproof side down on the ground and together they arranged the bedding, before they lied down together, staring up into the night sky. As the thin veil of clouds were slowly opening like a curtain above them, thousands of stars sparkled and shone against the velvety, deep purple sky. Sophie slid her hand into his and their warm fingers intertwined. He couldn't get enough of the sensation, and warmth filled him. "I'll never get over how beautiful it is," she whispered, and stared in wonder. "It makes me ponder what else I've missed, what else I was once blind to in the world."

He smiled, knowing the feeling all too well. He squeezed her hand while his thumb caressed over her knuckles. "Your eyes were open before. When you and I met that night at Howl at the Moon. You were the first woman who didn't flee at first sight when you saw my eyes."

She looked at him with a small smirk. "Maybe because of your suave pick up line."

He groaned. "That was definitely not my finest moment."

She laughed and turned to her side, her warm, soft body pressing against him. "Oh, I don't know. I think you made up for it with your rendition of Billy Joel's *'Uptown Girl'*. Even if it was Alex's prank."

He blushed, which only evoked another laugh from Sophie, and before he could respond, she leaned in closer and her soft lips pressed against his. She pulled away after a long moment, her green and gold eyes locked with his.

His heart raced and the primal look she gave him was both familiar and new. Her lips locked with his and she tasted him, again and again, and he was all too happy to be her captive for the moment, and for the night.

~*~

His mouth fit perfectly against hers. She heard his heartbeat speed up and her hand moved to his chest. Beneath his ribs his heart fluttered like a caged bird. She pinned him to the sleeping bag as their kiss deepened. When their lips parted, she inhaled his scent, which had taken a sweeter, intoxicating fragrance as he was turned on by her. Something about it only aroused her even more, being able to sense just how badly he wanted her. No, needed her.

She climbed into his lap, straddled him, and kissed him. She hadn't felt this amorous with anyone since she was a teenager, and yet it was so much more than lust driven by hormones. Sophie moaned against his mouth, and a new fire was suddenly lit within her, an ache and burn that came from deep inside, something she hadn't felt in a long time.

When they pulled away breathless from one another, she didn't let him get too far away. Their eyes were locked together, his lips inches from hers, his breath curled with hers. She knew what she wanted, and judging from his scent and the hardened bump beneath her, Korban wanted it too. She reached up and caressed his cheek as he leaned into her touch. "I want you," he said softly.

Never had those words touched her so deeply. There was only one thing to say in response to that. Perhaps two, but she blurted, "Show me."

He gave a soft growl as he leaned in, captured her lips once more with his own. When he pulled away this time, his voice was lower and hungry with desire. "Sophie…" The way he said her name sent a thrill through her body.

She bent down and kissed him again, before she slid her hands over his own and guided them up her thighs, resting his warm, strong hands at her hips. She kept her eyes locked on his as she peeled her borrowed t-shirt up over her head. His cheeks darkened and his breath hitched. She dropped the shirt somewhere behind her and guided his hands again. His fingers slid up her sides before bringing them to rest over her breasts. Her nipples hardened against his palms and she moaned softly, "Korban… touch me, taste me…" She felt him grow harder beneath her and she rocked her hips against him, which evoked another lustful moan from him.

At her encouragement his hands caressed her, explored her, caused her to arch up into his touch. He sat up and his mouth moved to her collar, kissed down her chest. She wanted… no needed more of him. Her fingers tugged and pulled his shirt up, breaking his mouth's contact with her skin as she tore his shirt off him with a lusty growl. She tossed it aside and cupped his face in her hands, drawing him in for another passionate kiss. Her hands ran over his feverish skin and he wrapped his arms around her. The cool night air was a delightful contrast to his hot skin.

He rolled her beneath him suddenly, which caused her to gasp in surprise. She found herself beneath him, her back sunk into the softness of the sleeping bag, barely feeling the hard ground beneath the material and the softness of the grass. His mouth briefly reunited with hers, before he began kissing and licking an erratic trail down her chin, throat, collar… his tongue trailed each soft pressure of his lips and she threaded her fingers through his short, dark hair, her body arching up to meet his questing mouth. She breathed in soft gasps, exhaled his name. Her heart pounded as his mouth captured her nipple and sucked on the hardened, sensitive nub.

His hands moved down her sides as he leaned in and kissed down her breast softly, which evoked a cry from deep inside of her. It had been awhile, but damn she had never wanted it so bad in her life before. His yellow eyes were filled with primal lust as he took in her scent through his nose. Her breasts were bared before him, and trembling as he leaned in, he caressed the underside of her bosom with a light brush of his fingertips, then his lips parted again and his tongue came out and teased her with a hot, wet lick over her sensitive skin. She yelped and arched into his touch, her legs wrapped around his waist, her fingers dug into his hair.

His scent was overwhelming and wonderful, his touch and tongue made her writhe against the ground. She'd wanted him so bad, perhaps as long as she had known him, and now to finally have him teasing her like this... it was a glorious victory, one she savored. She didn't have long to think about this as his lips surrounded her neglected right breast and he gave her other side the same treatment which only left her panting and aching for more. When he pulled away, the cold made her nipples tighten even more, and she pulled his face to hers and kissed him hungrily, her tongue darting to meet his inside his mouth.

Her hands moved down his bare back, marveling at the tight muscles that moved with his every touch, every breath. His lips moved from hers, then trailed back down her throat. She gasped as he nibbled lightly at the juncture of her neck and shoulder, the light scraping of teeth not painful but quite the opposite, the sensation sent tingles of pleasure all the way down to her toes.

Korban kissed down her body and sparked small fires where ever those talented lips touched, until he reached her borrowed sweatpants and gazed up to her. She stopped writhing and met those molten gold eyes, and she swore in that instant they were glowing, not just some trick of the moonlight above. He slid his fingertips beneath the elastic band of her pants and tugged the soft material down past her hips. When his eyes fell upon her jagged white scar on the pale skin of her hip, she blushed. For a moment, butterflies stirred nervously in her stomach as she felt embarrassed that maybe she wasn't perfect any more in his eyes. But those gold eyes never faltered, still smoldering with desire as he leaned in and licked the outside of her bite mark, the hyper-sensitive flesh near her scar causing that fiery tongue to ignite her senses all the more. The fire became white hot, almost electric, as he dipped lower still before she knew it, and then... his tongue was driving her wild, causing her to writhe against the sleeping bag. Her hands moved to his head again, getting tangled in his hair as the pleasure became overwhelming. Something was building within her, and the pleasure became almost unbearable. Her hands shook, uncertain of whether to push him away or pull him closer and let that pleasure reach blissful climax; something she hadn't visited in a long time.

She almost screamed when he suddenly pulled away, her body trembling and tense as his mouth returned to hers. Soft whines escaped her throat, and she reached down, quickly removed his pants and found him, heard his moan against her ear as she wrapped her fingers around his length, and tugged on him. He was so much hotter down here, so much thicker and longer than she had imagined. Sophie stroked him and his moans were a constant mantra in her ear. "Want you," she whispered into his ear, and nipped his earlobe, causing his solid erection to jump in her hand.

"Want you... too..." He was breathless, ready for her.

There was no more need for words, and as he positioned

himself, Sophie emitted a low guttural cry as he finally made contact with her entrance and he was inside of her.

She let the forest, no, the world know her pleasure at that moment, and her cries filled the air and drowned out any remaining music of the night. His own cries were the only other thing she could hear, besides the racing of their hearts in time. When she climbed to the very peak of her pleasure she didn't simply fall, but flew. A white-hot explosion that she never felt as intensely before suddenly wiped the world away, and for a moment all she knew was ecstasy.

When the world came back into focus again, he was holding her close, his body pressed flush against hers. She clung to him, her mouth near his throat, his heart echoing in her ear. She could smell only him, feel only him, and taste him on her tongue. At this moment he was everything, and she loved him more than she could say.

"I love you," Korban murmured to her as he nuzzled her throat and drew her closer into his embrace.

At his words she smiled, opened her mouth to say those words back, but they caught in her throat. His breathing had leveled out, his arm went limp alongside her as he nestled closer against her. Her own weariness set in, the adrenaline and exhilaration of their lovemaking fading to the blissful feeling of contentment of just cuddling up with him. She rested her head on his chest as the sounds of the night suddenly began to lightly crescendo once more around her, and the lullaby of the forest along with his steady heartbeat, lulled her off to a sweet, dreamless sleep.

6: CAUGHT

The next several days passed by like a dream. An erotic, steamy dream that seemed more fantasy than reality, especially so distanced from the world they knew. Now that they had opened up to one another, there was suddenly not enough hours in the day to do everything they wanted together, or so it seemed.

She couldn't get enough of him, and he couldn't get enough of her. The morning after their first time was like a second honeymoon, followed by countless times after that. After a while, it was almost as if they had become one person, one being. Even their scents intertwined long after their bodies had separated.

They lay together breathless, and she smiled to him, running a hand through his messy mane of hair. He leaned into her touch, looking extremely content and satisfied. Her heart was still racing, her body tingling and on fire, though the full moon was approaching now and her feverish skin was an everyday thing.

His mouth curved into his trademark lop-sided smile, his amber eyes bright with an array of golden hues. She studied him for a long, quiet moment as they caught their breath.

I love you.

He'd said those three words that made her heart soar. The way he looked at her she had no doubt that he meant them, no question about it. So why was she still afraid to repeat them back to him?

"Tomorrow night is the full moon, and we have one more direction to check out. I have a feeling we'll find our way back home. Then after the full moon... we can rest, and when we're ready we can go." Korban's voice was weary, but relaxed. Relieved.

She smiled and nodded to him as her fingers curled in his hair and rubbed his scalp behind his ear, the action causing his eyes to roll back in pleasure. His response pleased her; something about knowing him so well that she knew how to push his buttons just right... it made her feel good, empowered. "I don't care where we end up, as long as I am with you," she said softly.

I love you.

She tried but the words seemed to get stuck in her throat. She leaned in and they kissed, which made her heart flutter anew. When they broke away a few moments later, she caught a glimpse of worry in his eyes, and her hand moved to his cheek. "Tell me what's wrong," she said, as her fingers curled to cup his face.

He flashed a nervous smile, but it faded quickly. He already knew he couldn't hide anything from her. "I... I don't really want to go back," he confessed, his face crumpled with a mournful, apologetic look. "I'm afraid they're going to put you... and me... in quarantine. They could separate us, or perform more tests on us. Especially because of that... poison, chemical, whatever it was that forced us to shift." He paused and took a breath, then continued with a hushed voice, filled with shame. "We have to go back, or they'll throw RJ in jail, and they'll never let him out no matter what he says or does. It will be all my fault for leaving and not reporting in. The stupid law is clear on that. He will be punished as my legal sponsor if I'm not under his care. But the thought of us disappearing together like this… to never have to go back… it would be so easy to just vanish." She petted his cheek with her thumb as tears welled in his eyes. "I just… I can't do that to RJ and Alex, not after everything they have done. They're my best friends, more like my brothers really. My family. I feel horrible just thinking about it, abandoning them like that. But I won't lie to you, it's so damn tempting."

She felt him tremble as fear rolled off him. Fear of quarantine, which he still seemed uncomfortable to talk about. A place of untold horrors. Fear of losing his humanity, of betraying his Pack that waited back home for him. She understood those fears, because they were hers as well. They could return home only to be tossed into some asylum and never be seen or heard from again. "I'm scared of going back too," she said as she held his gaze. "We will face a lot, but we will do it together. When we go back we can set things right. It won't be the end of the world. We are survivors."

He smiled then, the light returning to his eyes. Just as he was her rock, she knew in that moment that she was his too. Still, those three words evaded her lips, so instead she did the next best thing and leaned in to kiss him again.

His hands slid to her hips and she was lost in their kiss, and any doubts were chased away for now. Soon enough they would be back to reality, back where they couldn't hide from the past. For now it was okay to get swept up in this delightful fantasy.

~*~

A couple hours before the full moon, they parted ways from their camp just in case someone decided to return that unfortunate night. They hiked through the forest, around the lake's edge, and up over rocky paths that crumbled under their feet. The clearing they finally stopped at was peaceful, the scents purely wild. Earth, water, and musky animal. No one human had set foot up there in a very long time.

Korban set down the backpack he'd found and gazed to her, the sky behind him a series of pinks and purples, from lavender to the rich royal purple. The colors complimented the vibrant yellow glow of his eyes. It was almost time; the churning inside her body had already begun. The feeling was akin to menstrual cramps, only it spread deeper through her bones, all over her body. She slipped her hand into Korban's and his touch soothed the ache. It still hurt like hell, but having him next to her made the pain at least somewhat bearable.

They stripped off their clothes, then packed them into the borrowed backpack and hung it up on a low-hanging tree branch. The air was cool but her skin felt hot, then comfortably warm, as his skin made contact with hers again. It wasn't sexual as she held him this close to her while naked… it wasn't completely platonic either, but something much deeper in between. She felt safe, even as those first agonizing spasms took hold, as her bones snapped, and when molten lava took the place of the blood in her veins. She felt his body shuddering as his own Change took hold… there came a time when their hands stopped holding, their skin stopped touching, but he was still right there beside her and it was as if he still did have his hand in hers.

~*~

When the pain had subsided, leaving his muscles and body trembling in its wake, he slowly opened his eyes. The forest was even more vibrant; the smells more intense than before, but of everything in the fragrant air around them, the one familiar scent remained familiar. His Mate, his home. He lifted his head and saw her panting there beside him, her soft, golden fur speckled by the moonlight that slipped through the thick canopy of trees up above them. His legs quivered when he got up on them, adjusting from two legs to four. His tail held his balance, and he managed not to fall flat on his face. He slowly moved over to her. She was already on her feet by the time he made it over, shaking herself. Those familiar, yellow eyes gleamed, and her tail gave a small wag. It was his Mate, and while the familiar scents of the garage weren't around, her presence made him feel at home. The breeze suddenly shook through the trees, sending an array of new smells, things unfamiliar and new.

She moved closer to him, brushing against his side, her shoulder touching his. He lifted his head and sniffed the air, tensing alongside her. He relaxed when nothing dangerous caught his attention, then moved and sniffed her over, making sure she was all right. She stood still as he did, her heart racing. Playfully, she nipped at his ear, and he jerked his head up in surprise. She chuffed heartily at him and bounced back, suddenly remembering and then nimble on her feet once more. She bowed and wagged her tail, getting comfortable in her new skin. The primal part of her was finally freed again from its prison of human skin and two-legged rules. She yipped playfully, and suddenly tore off, giving him a quick glance as she raced off into the forest. The chase was on. He could hear her heart, and feel the rush of wind through his fur as he rushed after her, his foot falls nearly silent on the soft forest floor. She sped up, the thrill of the chase sending adrenaline through his body, leaping over fallen logs, splashing through the small creeks they passed.

She slowed when the sound of water rushing grew louder, and he caught up, licking her ear and giving her fur a series of playful nips. She nudged him and bowed her head, sniffed the water and found nothing foreign in it, nothing that smelled dangerous to her anyway, and she began to lap up the cool water. He moved alongside her and joined her in drinking from the river. It tasted wonderful.

A very two-legged idea suddenly bubbled from her mind. She waited and suddenly leapt at him, knocking him unexpectedly into the water with a huge splash. She fell in after him, laughter coming out in chuffs as she emerged from the water dripping along the bank.

He got up and shook the water from his fur, blinking as he

jerked his head to her in surprise. He gave a small playful yip and growl, and then took off after her, causing her to turn and run. The chase was on again.

The freedom of the forest, of running free with his Mate... it was so exhilarating. Here they had no worries, only the now. Sudden bursts of speed made him leap forward, moving faster. His muscles ached and burned from the run but it felt so amazing, so liberating, he didn't want to stop. She was incredibly fast, and as always, her stamina seemed to burst past him. She is like lightning again, one foot away from him, then two, then more, and as fast as he chased she was faster.

They reached a small clearing where she bolted ahead, him rushing to keep up with her. There was a snap beneath him and a sudden dip in the earth, and before he could help it, he found himself falling as the ground beneath him gave away and caved in. With a loud yelp he vanished from her heels, the rush of leaves, grass and mud collapsing beneath him as the ground vanished beneath his paws. The next thing he knew he was yanked hard as thick ropes surrounded him, stopping his fall and tangling around him like snakes.

The dirt and foliage fell around him in a whirlwind of debris that stuck to his still damp fur. He tried to get to his feet but the ropes tangled even more around him, and when he tried to push off the ground he found only air. Another few feet remained below him as he hung from this web of rope. He lifted his head up. Above him were tall, spread-out stone and brick walls, and beyond that, the clear night sky was dotted with bright stars.

He grunted and struggled to get some sort of foot hold, but instead swayed pathetically, the net groaning under his weight but not giving way, not budging down even an inch. A soft whimper came from above and his attention moved to his Mate, who peered down worriedly at him. Somehow she had made it across this pit he now dangled over. She began to pace along the edge of the trap, carefully treading along the edges, trying to find a way to help him out of peril.

There suddenly came a series of howls nearby... and a chill ran through him. Those were not wolves. Korban struggled more violently, but found it useless and barked to her, *Run!*

~*~

She lurched to run, but hesitated. She pleaded with him, not wanting to leave him there, and a long whine escaped her. Not like this, not where he was vulnerable and alone and—

RUN! His gaze was on her as he barked sharply, and despite her will being so strong, with a whimper of protest she took off, whining with every step. He was her Mate, but his wolf was her Alpha. Her two-legged brain was trying to understand, to figure a way to free him, but at the urgency of his tone she could not disobey. Her only option was to run, to get help. To come back and rescue him.

She had to hurry; she had to get help as fast as possible. Those howls came again and they were closer now, and made her freeze in her tracks. That urgency grew inside of her still, stronger with every moment that passed. She had to run. She doubled back the way they came, splashed through the river, back up the path... the river rounded back through, and she became disoriented... this wasn't the right way. This couldn't be right. The scents here were new, and she couldn't find the trail she'd blazed with her Mate. She circled around, sniffing... but the water had erased her path, and she'd been running so fast she couldn't place where she'd come from anymore.

Those haunting howls erupted once more from the mountain, but they were further away this time. Her heart was pounding in her skull. The sky was lightening again, and night would soon give way to the day, and she had to get back to her Mate before then, before she was naked and helpless as a two-legger again, left blind and deaf and weakened from the subsiding power of the moon. She could howl for him, but that would draw attention from the others back towards her, and she didn't want that. What if they had found her Mate, helpless and hanging in that awful trap? She threw her head back and howled to him, and their howls came again in response.

No! She couldn't think of the number, but she knew that they greatly outnumbered her and her Mate. Still, she could run, and as their howls grew closer, she tore off again, splashed once more through the river, steering them hopefully away from where her Mate was trapped. Cornered, he didn't stand a chance against them. But she was fast and surefooted. She could easily lead them where she wanted for the night. When she was two-legged again, she could return with help and get him out of that hole. She only hoped that the wolves chasing her weren't faster than she was.

~*~

His leg was twisted beneath him, excruciating pain shooting through it, and he struggled to get his weight off it, to shift it somehow, but it was impossible. The net was too tight around him, and one foot dangled outside of it. At least his Mate was safe, and far away from there. He struggled again but to no avail. He tried a new tactic and attempted to bite through the rope, gnawing on it, but something intertwined with the rope burned his tongue, caused him to yelp and pull back. The silver strands glistened in the moonlight, and he sneezed, huffed to get that burning sensation off his tongue. The howls began again, this time much closer... too close. He froze, ignored the flaring ache of his leg and watched, listening as something approached.

Above him, an unfamiliar wolf was watching, carefully skirting along the edge of the hole. He felt a defensive growl rumble from his own throat, but he cut it short. He was in no position to challenge anyone at the moment, but his warning was made clear.

Another wolf appeared, larger, and had a matching pale gold color in the moonlight. They saw him swinging helpless down there and chuffed at the other wolf, who whined softly. Something suddenly crashed through the trees and the two of them took a few steps back... a third wolf with darker colored fur skidded to a halt alongside them, and then he heard his Mate's howl, and nothing else mattered. His Mate was calling to him, and he couldn't even call back to her. If she came now... what would these other wolves do to her?

He growled again, but they weren't interested in her howl, it seemed. Something about the way the gathered wolves watched him stuck in the trap seemed to radiate sympathy before another chorus of howls filled the air from the distance and they suddenly turned and left him there. Alone.

He whimpered helplessly. The sky was turning light again, the moon's power already fading. His leg ached painfully. It was going to hurt even more when the Change came once more. He closed his eyes and prayed that his Mate was in a much safer place; maybe somewhere she could find help.

7: STRANGERS

When Sophie woke she was curled tightly into herself, the cold air of the morning brushing her backside. She nestled back, hoping to make contact with his warm body but Korban wasn't there. She shivered, confused for a moment as she struggled to remember something from the night before but it was all hazy, like a faded dream she could barely recall.

"Korban...?" her voice was raspy. No response came.

She tried to get her bearings as she sat up and scanned the area with her weary eyes, but nothing looked familiar in this stretch of forest. What was worse, her senses were dulled down to normal after the climax of the full moon, and she couldn't rely on her keen nose to find the path. Her hearing wasn't as reliable either, and the birds chirping and the river bubbling nearby were the only sounds she picked up. She stood slowly, and her knees weakly buckled at her first steps. She didn't see Korban in the area, and her heart sank.

All the tall trees around her looked the same, towering evergreens, maples, and oaks. Their sweet smells were the same, and her own trail went in frantic circles. It seemed hopeless, but she was not one to give up, especially now. She had to find Korban.

There was a fleeting moment where she wished she could find their bag of clothes, but compared to all of her other problems at the moment, covering her nakedness was a minor issue. Once she was on her feet she briefly missed having shoes, but at least the ground here was soft and mossy, damp with morning dew. Her eyes came to focus on a massive set of paw prints in the mud. For a moment she stared in wonder. Her eyes followed the path they made and they headed up to where she had rested. Her paw prints. The thought that the strange markings belonged to her wolf was even more surreal as they were irrevocable proof of what she'd been last night, in case her aching body wasn't enough of a reminder. She tried to call to him again, this time a little louder. "Korban?" There was still no answer, so she looked to where her wolf tracks entered the area and started to retrace her trail back. Perhaps she would spot his tracks as well and find where he had ended up. She wished more than anything that she could remember something, anything from the night before, but her memory remained a blank as she followed the steps back through the thick brush of this untouched forest.

As she followed the paw prints, she suddenly heard voices up ahead. Sophie froze and listened. Her heart sank when she realized the voices that were grumbling and yawning did not belong to her missing Mate. For a moment, she couldn't make out what they were saying, the voices gruff but quiet, as if they sensed an audience lurking from the trees nearby. Maybe they were campers, which meant help and at least – hopefully – clothes. She would have to quickly come up with a reason for being naked out in the middle of the woods, but as she approached and peered tentatively around the cover of the trees and bushes, she realized she didn't have to worry about it. Her cheeks went hot again as she averted her gaze to the scene she'd stumbled upon. The group of men there were as stark naked as she was, and were all getting dressed in hushed whispers. Whatever she had walked up on, she didn't want to know.

"We have to get moving. I remember seeing a wolf trapped last night," a female's voice suddenly piped up over the grumbles of the men. Sophie paused, listening. Did these people set a trap that Korban fell into? Her hand clenched into a fist at the thought. She didn't care how many of them there were, or if they were stronger than her and more dressed. She'd do whatever it took to get Korban back safely with her, where he belonged. "Finish dressing and let's get on the move. We don't have much time."

Sophie growled softly at that, simultaneously stepping on a branch and snapping it. The grumbles went silent. "Someone's there," a not too bright sounding man growled softly.

Shit.

~*~

Korban woke, his arm burning with pain and other aches shooting throughout his body. The air was cold and the rope was making him itch. His skin was raw and red from the impressions caused by his own weight. He groaned, feeling incredibly weak as his head spun. He remembered everything clearly, running with Sophie, then falling and getting snagged in this terrible trap... and now, something besides the pain had woke him. Sophie... where was Sophie? He opened his mouth to call out to her when something else caught his attention. A low growl in the distance echoed around him, a mechanical sound that seemed to be getting louder, and soon the rumble of an engine became a roar as the vehicle approached.

He could easily talk this out. Whoever set this trap was probably looking for a bear or something like that. They'd all laugh when they saw him hanging there naked, then pull him out of this pit and he'd even be generous enough to just walk away without incident. Hopefully, that's what would happen. He wasn't that badly hurt, just very uncomfortable and wanted to go home and take a soak in the lake with Sophie... oh no. Sophie must be worried sick about him. He'd told her to run for help. Was that maybe her returning with someone? He heard the engine rumbling nearby, up in the clearing above him now. He struggled to get into a more dignified position as a metallic squeak signaled brakes grinding to a halt, followed by a masculine grunt as someone opened a heavy metal door. Heavy footsteps approached the pit.

His aching arm gave a small throb of hope when two men in camouflage jumpsuits and hats suddenly peered down at him from the edge of the pit. Now he would be freed and finally have a good laugh about this. One of the men looked menacing, a permanent frown etched on his face, square jaw clenched and covered in cropped, pale whiskers. He carried himself like a drill sergeant, and was built like one, tall with lean muscle. The other man looked like he was barely out of high school, thin and stringy with a long neck and beady eyes. His eyes bulged a little and he shifted around anxiously when he saw Korban caught in their trap.

"Thank goodness you guys are here now; I accidentally stumbled upon your trap, funny story…" Confusion set in, quickly replaced by horror when he saw the drill sergeant nod to the kid next to him, and the skinny boy pulled some sort of rifle from his shoulder and pointed it down at him.

Korban's eyes widened in terror and he quickly stammered, "Wait! Please... I... I didn't mean to trespass or anything, I-!"

There was a loud click then the sound of rushing air, and something sharp stuck him hard in the arm. Korban had a moment to stare at his arm, the syringe poking deep into his flesh and some sort of liquid vanished into his bloodstream. Fear gripped him. He only had a few seconds to wonder what the hell just happened–

And then his vision swam as his eyes rolled up into his head, and the world went black and silent.

~*~

Footsteps approached and Sophie ducked behind a bush, crouched to cover herself, and prepared to spring, when a burly blonde woman suddenly peered over the bushes at her, her hair falling in curly strands over her shoulders. She was wearing a black t-shirt and jeans, and while she was big and curvy it wasn't just soft fat. She was large and curvy in a way that was muscular and strong. Her nostrils flared and her yellow-gold eyes widened in surprise. Wolf-like eyes, just like Korban's. Sophie tensed and her nostrils flared. "Stop." The woman told the other guys, and then her expression softened. "You look familiar. Who are you?"

Sophie was taken aback. These men and this woman were also werewolves. She stammered in response. "S-Sophie," she couldn't help it, it was in her breeding to have manners, even if confronted naked out in the woods by a pack of werewolves.

"Sophie Bane." Recognition dawned on the blonde's face. "Ahh... I see. Still well enough to transform back, that's good." She glanced to the others. "Grab the spare clothes, toss them to me." She barked the orders and then offered a smile to Sophie once more. "I'm Valkyrie, Val if you like. Sorry, we didn't expect to run into anyone else out here. Campers don't usually stay on the hiking trails this far away from civilization."

"Nice to meet you Val. I'm looking for my boyfriend Korban," her voice trembled a little with worry, "he was running with me last night. He was with me but we got separated somehow, have you seen him?"

Val gazed to her and gave a short nod. "We saw a wolf we didn't know caught in a pit, we just have to retrace our steps but I think we can find it." One of the guys tossed her a bag of clothes, a pair of dark sweat pants and a dark t-shirt, and she tossed it over to Sophie. "Get dressed hon and we'll get moving."

"Thank you," Sophie said gratefully, then quickly pulled on the clothes. She could deal without shoes for now. She was thankful to have her body covered from the cool morning air, and any of those large men's roving eyes. The looks she got when she did make her way from behind the bushes were bad enough.

She was used to the stares, or should have been by now. The wealthy housewife now turned monster, it was something the tabloids would have a field day with in each issue when she returned home. She was the first famous werewolf victim. She regarded the others anxiously as they finished dressing and putting on their boots, leather and spikes adorning much of their clothes. There were three large men who accompanied Val in the middle of the forest. A young, muscular man was pulling his long, dark brown hair back into a ponytail, another older, thin man covering his salt and pepper curls with a green bandana. They each wore identical leather cut vests with wolf skull insignias stitched onto the back that read *Valhalla Knights.*

Val was now standing next to the third man, whose arms were the size of small tree trunks, thick muscle that was lined with tattoo sleeves to each of his shoulders. He wasn't just solidly built; he was tall, even taller than the large woman and the other two men who were standing there. His blond hair was equally as long, if not as thick as hers, and his beard was neatly trimmed short, close to the skin. His gaze pierced through his dark sunglasses as he offered an amicable smile. "Sophie freaking Bane. Well this turned out to be a pleasant surprise. I'm the pack leader, Odin," he paused and put an arm around Val as his eyebrows raised in mild amusement. "You're definitely not as dead as the rumors claim you to be. Devoured by a werewolf... well, looks like those rumors may be slightly exaggerated."

Giving her names like Odin and Valkyrie, she wondered if they were hiding something, or if maybe their pack went by nicknames. They were out here in the wild after all, with no human sponsors to be seen. "Yeah, you can say that again," She impatiently looked around. They were still strangers after all, and she wanted to get to Korban as quickly as possible. Nothing was moving fast enough for her, and she did not want to appear ungrateful for the clothing, but she wanted to run to Korban and get him out of that trap and home before something bad happened.

"You're prettier than those pictures in the magazines," the man with the ponytail commented, not in a lewd or leering way, but she recognized the voice as the one who'd spoken earlier. He gave a charming grin, or it would have been if it didn't painfully remind her of Korban.

"Thank you," Sophie said, glancing to the tall blond couple since they appeared to be the ones in charge. "I don't mind talking more, and I don't want to be rude, but my Mate may be stuck in a pit at the moment and I want to get to him before whoever set that trap gets there. I'm sure you understand."

Valkyrie nodded. "We should hurry. We don't want to lose a lead like this."

They started walking in the direction they believed they had seen the wolf trap, and Sophie quickly rushed up to follow them. She was curious about what they meant by a "lead" but only a little bit. More than anything she wanted to get to Korban, so they could all laugh this off later. She kept her distance, just in case this was a trap in itself... after all, no one seemed to be polite enough to offer a real name in return yet, and they knew she was some sort of macabre celebrity survivor. Who knew what was running through the minds of these werewolves? She was trying not to be prejudiced, but her inner wolf, though sated from the moon, was still anxious and suspicious. Regardless of who they were as humans, they were still a foreign wolf pack, and she was in unfamiliar territory— both which were dangerous to her until she was reunited with Korban again.

8: CAPTIVES

Korban's skull throbbed in time with his racing heartbeat when he woke. His mouth was dry and the only thing that hurt worse than his head was his arm. Before he could even see where he was, the smell hit him. Even with his senses dulled, the stench was overwhelming: a stomach churning mixture of sewage, blood, and cheap cologne. It made him gag, and a voice next to him said in a crisp British accent, "Breathe through your mouth, mate. It helps a bit."

He took their advice, whoever they were, and it did help- at least a little. "Thanks," he croaked, then finally managed to open his eyes and focus on where he was now. His vision swam and came to focus on... silver bars?

The cement ground was cold and smooth beneath him. As he glanced around he saw silver bars on every side of him, surrounding him. It was far too small to be a jail cell... it was almost the size of a crate for a large dog. Or a human being.

His eyes adjusted to the darkness, and he suppressed a gasp of alarm. Throughout the room, there were other cages like his. Laying in many of those human-sized crates were shadowy figures that he couldn't quite make out. Was he dreaming? Or worse, was this some kind of purgatory? No... that disgusting smell was too real to be some dream, the pain too intense in his arm and head to be some state of death. The closest experience he had was when he'd been attacked and bitten five years ago. That had been almost a peaceful, floating experience after the sharp wolf teeth tore and ripped into his collar. It definitely wasn't like this harsh and raw feeling.

He remembered the net, then the needle sticking in his arm. The two masked men...

So like the last time. Only their surgical masks were blue or white, and he'd been bound in the dark room to a hospital bed by his wrists and ankles, unable to escape-

No, no, no. He couldn't go through the tests again. All the poking and prodding...

He scrambled to the back of his prison and almost instantly regretted the move. It was as if the bars were on fire and scorched his skin instantly upon contact. He cried out and fell forward, gasping for breath. "What the hell?!"

"Silver bars. Not just coated either. Pure, solid silver." The same clipped British voice spoke softly in a hushed whisper. "Keep your voice down or you'll draw attention."

"I hope the hell I do!" Korban growled. "Who are they to think they can stuff me into– us into—" he quickly remedied, "—some cage like an animal?!"

A quieter, anxious male voice across the room pleaded, "Please, please don't! Don't provoke *Them*!" The last word held more emphasis and fear than most villains or terrorists did.

"Them? Who are they?" Korban asked, but suddenly there was the sound of a heavy metal click.

A lock being unlocked not too far away and the softest, scared voice whimpered, "Oh no..."

Heavy footsteps echoed and scuffed menacingly beyond the unseen door. Korban felt a growl build in his throat that had nothing to do with being a werewolf. It was cut short when a bright light suddenly flooded the room and a heavy door creaked open. He squinted, still blinded as his eyes readjusted from the darkness to light.

The shadowy figure that came into focus was wearing dark grey and black camouflage, just like the two who had shot him with the dart in the net trap. Their stature and build was tall and solid, very square. Obviously masculine, even though they were covered from head to toe, from a dark ski mask down to their shiny, black polished combat boots. More than likely the drill sergeant who'd been frowning down at him. Any attention to the attire was instantly lost when he saw the rifle in the masked man's hands. It looked like something military issued, the kind Korban had seen before only in the movies.

The stink of heavy cologne surrounded the man, as if he was even covering his scent from them. The thought sent a cold chill down Korban's spine.

Maybe it was the drugs finally clearing out of his system, or perhaps it was this armed, masked man who sobered him up and woke up his brain. Regardless, the light bulb clicked on as he put it all together. The pit and its painful net, with its glinting silver inside the thick rope. The strange tranquilizing dart in his arm. The silver bars, solid and thick around his cage. That trap hadn't been just for a bear, or even the smallest chance of capturing a natural wolf. These men around him, in their own silver bound cages, no doubt, were caught in the same cruel trap. Even with the reek of strong cologne and sewage covering it up, he was sure he could smell the hint of many other wolves. The men in the cages, they were infected too. Werewolves like him.

But why would these people capture werewolves, risking their own lives or risking infection upon themselves, to bring them here to this place?

All of his questions spun around in his brain, and came to a thunderous halt when he found himself staring down the barrel of a gun once again.

His heart went up to his throat but he glared defiantly into the eyes of the gun man. He would not die here cowering like some kicked pup.

The eyes that peered from the slits of the ski mask were a cold, dull black-brown. No emotion reflected in those flat eyes, but they were clearly calculating, as if sizing Korban up. He suddenly didn't care about the frightened werewolf's previous warning. Not that he was ever one to be bothered by such things as keeping his mouth shut. "Who the hell do you think you are, putting men in cages like this? You'd better let us go right now, before the authorities discover this false prison, or so help me if I get my hands on you—"

There was a thunderous bang and he jumped back, his ears ringing. The gun was aimed at him again and the man squeezed the trigger. He fired it once again, the bullet striking into the cement next to him. A bit of silver had melted to the ground where the bullet struck, and Korban stared at it, then returned his gaze to the gun man once more, stunned. "Who the hell are you people?" Silver was understandably more expensive than gold these days.

The gun man stared at him for a long moment then smirked, but there was no humor in his eyes. Just a flash of surprise, then a stony, cold stare as he studied him. Even more infuriating, the man said nothing as he stood there and stared him down, and then moved to the next cage, which in the light Korban saw were all lined up in a large circle.

As he frantically searched for some way to escape, he took in his surroundings, keeping his silent captor within his sight as he took it in. There were six cages, including the medium-sized one he was in, evenly spread out in a circle within what looked like a windowless warehouse room. Fluorescent lights and flood lights shone brightly down upon them and illuminated the plain, drywall panels that lined the walls of the room. Cement sealed the bottoms of their cages, but beyond the silver bars the ground was mostly dirt, some patches of hay lighting some areas, while some areas appeared to be darkened by something more foul. Of the six cages, four were occupied, much to Korban's horror. Three strangers were stuck just like him, all three of them werewolves, though he could only tell this by their scent. Like Sophie, their eyes had returned to a human guise now that the full moon had been sated.

They sat and glanced around but mostly kept their gazes down as their masked captor circled their small prisons. Two of the men appeared to be older than he was; the one in the crate to his left in particular had his eyes focused intently on the floor. The man had a weary, haggard appearance, his military style cut hair light gray, with small flecks of dark hairs here and there.

The older man who crouched in the crate across from him was a chubby, grizzly man with faded tattoos that adorned his body and a wild look in his eyes. He had a thick, salt and pepper beard and clutched a thin blanket in his hands, nervously picking at a loose thread and wincing as the masked man approached his cage.

The man remained silent as he made his way around their assembled cages. He tapped the side of the grizzly man's cage with the butt of his rifle, making a loud, ringing clang that caused the werewolf within to yelp out in a very human manner and clutch his blanket closer, his knuckles turning white as he cowered. This evoked a cruel, barking chortle from him, but he still said nothing as he finished his patrol past the third man, a man about Korban's age who glared up at the stranger who passed his crate, squaring his jaw but saying nothing as his pale blue eyes sent a look that would make a more squeamish man run in the other direction.

No one was saying anything, and Korban bit his tongue to keep from growling out again in frustration. He was certain if he pushed his luck this jerk would put a silver bullet in him instead of the floor next time. How long had this been going on? Why were they being held prisoner like this? What purpose did this serve? With no answers from their silent captor, he could only hope to get answers from the others once he left. The masked man leveled his rifle again, this time pointing it at the defiant werewolf's head. Korban's eyes widened as he watched the gun man's finger twitch on the trigger.

The doors on the other side of the large room creaked open and a second man strode into the room, smaller and thinner but wearing the same uniform as the other man, and drenched in that same heavy cologne. Most likely the boy from before who'd tranquilized him, by the look of his long neck. Korban wanted to wring his scrawny throat. "What's wrong?" he demanded sharply, his voice just as thin and trembling as his lanky body.

"New dog was out of line. I put him in his place." The larger one lowered his rifle then nodded in Korban's direction, his voice a deep grumble and just as unpleasant as his barking laugh.

The smaller man grumbled as he glanced his way. "The boss is gonna be pissed you wasted a bullet for nothin'..." He suddenly stopped and gave Korban a curious look. "Huh. That new one is different from the others. That'll amuse the boss."

"Maybe then he won't be mad about the bullet, huh?" The larger one sounded somewhat hopeful at the prospect.

"Maybe," the smaller man repeated, then jabbed the larger man in the arm. "Let's go talk to 'im. He should know."

"Right." They turned to leave and headed for the door.

Korban knew two things for sure. Whatever it was that made him different from the rest made him valuable from the sounds of things, at least to this boss of theirs anyway. And he also knew, when a boss was involved, or any higher up, he wouldn't be killed until the orders were given.

Besides, he was even more pissed knowing that this was some sort of team operation, and he didn't appreciate being called a dog. Only Alex got away with the nickname he'd dubbed him, "Lobo."

"Who's in charge of this?" Korban yelled as he boldly moved closer to the bars and stared both of the men down. "Let the coward show his face!"

The smaller man paused and gave Korban a look. "This ain't exactly a democracy here, pal. In case the silver bars and bullets weren't enough for you to understand."

"You can't just cage men like this! We have rights!" Korban snarled, and the others perked up in their crates, watching the shouting bout like a tennis match.

Amusement lit the larger one's eyes as the smaller one snickered. "Men. Last I knew, werewolves were monsters."

"That was when we weren't the real deal! When the only werewolves you saw were pretend!" Korban tried a different approach. "Five years ago I was just a man, I didn't ask for this! I bet no one here did!"

"Boo hoo," the smaller one taunted, then rolled his eyes. "Regardless, you're here now. And you're not going anywhere until the boss says otherwise. Sorry Charlie. No bones for bad dogs."

"Wait! You can't just leave us here!" Korban watched as they started to leave again. No, no... he had to make them angry enough to do something stupid. Then he could try to escape...

But no matter what he yelled, what obscenity he tried, they ignored him and left. Frustrated he rammed his hands against the bars but instantly regretted the move as the white-hot metal seared his flesh. He yelped and fell back, then glared at the doors even when the lights shut down and the darkness blinded him once again.

~*~

They carefully trudged through the forest, moving as quietly as they could as a group. Sophie tried to keep a safe distance as she was still wary of the wolf pack, but it seemed that she'd caught the unwanted attention of the youngest man there, the one with the mischievous smile that reminded her of Korban, named Freki. She kept her gaze focused ahead as he walked alongside her, but after they covered some ground he attempted to strike up a conversation. "So... this boyfriend of yours, are you two pretty serious? I mean... could a guy like me have a chance?"

Sophie shot him a death glare and Odin laughed as Freki leapt backward and found himself tangled up in some of the overgrowth surrounding a decaying tree. "Pardon our youngest pack brother's lack of manners. His older brother usually keeps him in line but we had Geri out on patrol last night to watch over our den."

Sophie's stern look sobered a little as the names clicked in place. "Odin, Valkyrie, Freki, Geri and," she looked to the third man there, who kept close to Odin and Valkyrie's side, "Skoll... all characters from Norse mythology."

"Beauty and brains? I think I'm in love," Freki sighed as he brushed the leaves and twigs away from his shoulders, only to have Val shoot him a look.

"Behave, Freki," she warned, though the harsh words were followed by a smirk. "I'm confident that you can take him out easily,

Sophie, but right now we have no time to waste. If we can find Korban maybe we'll find—"

Odin held up his hand suddenly and she stopped. He stared up ahead and gestured with a finger to his lips. They went silent and still, listening. Odin moved cautiously ahead, and as he did he motioned for them to stay, though Sophie moved closer to see what he had discovered, her heart racing, her ears straining and nose sniffing for clues.

A clearing opened up before them, almost out of nowhere. There was a feeling of déjà vu, like she'd been here before, and she couldn't shake it. Odin walked out, stepping lightly. A huge, rectangular hole opened up ahead of him, too geometric to be natural. The gaping hole triggered a memory, hazy and faded from the back of her mind. Running on four legs, scrambling, trying not to fall… then gazing down into another hole like this. A hole where her gray wolf had fallen, was caught in a net and couldn't escape. "Korban!" She breathed his name, rushed past the others, and moving to Odin's side, peered down into the pit.

Her heart sank as she stared down into the empty hole. What was worse, there wasn't even the faintest whiff of Korban's scent to confirm that this had been where he was trapped. At least not to her now human nose.

Frustration and panic began to build inside of her. They'd been wandering the forest for hours now, only to find this empty clearing where Korban might not have even been in. She could only hope that maybe, by some slim chance, he'd gotten free and was back at the trailer, waiting for her, or maybe even out there in the forest looking for her. Something inside of her was telling her this was wrong. Someone had set that trap strong enough not for just a wild animal. Korban was strong enough to easily break free of a regular hunter's trap. One that was designed to keep a werewolf in it, however…

She couldn't help it. Part of her wanted to scream in rage, the other part wanted to cry. She couldn't lose it, not now, but feeling this helpless and lost for the first time since he'd been there for her after the attack...

No. She couldn't lose it, and she wouldn't. She had to find Korban, and to find Korban she needed to think. Her other senses may have been dulled, but her mind was always her strongest asset, any time of the month.

If this was the place, any clue was valuable. She turned to Odin, whose expression was grim, his mouth a thin line as he glared down at the hole before them. "You're missing your pack mate, and so are we. Skoll's brother Hati has been missing since two full moons ago. Which is why we are here, this deep in the Adirondacks. We don't leave a brother behind." He paused and glanced to her. "I wasn't sure of it before, but this... I don't believe in coincidences. My gut was telling me before something sinister had happened with Hati, and this confirms it."

Sophie's eyes widened at his revelation, a fresh fear filled her as his words sunk in. "So you've been looking for your missing pack mate for over two months now?"

Odin nodded and gazed to Skoll, who was standing at the edge of the clearing, a pained look in his eyes. "Is this bringing back any memories? Anything familiar at all?"

He robotically nodded. "I remember Hati and me running, and then the ground... swallowed him up."

Another chill crept down her spine and Sophie wrapped her arms around herself. "That's all I remember too, Korban and I were running and then... he fell, too." She turned to the others and stepped away from the pit as her hair began to stand on end. "You've been searching for a couple months out here with no clues as to where your pack mate ended up?"

Odin sighed and nodded, rubbing his chin as his frown only continued to grow. "It's been frustrating as hell. Only a few of us can recall the full moon night. Myself and Val mostly, though Geri's memories have become stronger since we started. Skoll wasn't able to remember what happened to his brother. We've searched the area since Hati's disappearance but we weren't even really sure what to look for. But this… this is a huge lead. Finding you and now this wolf pit… this will shine some light as to what happened to Hati. And I suppose your Korban too."

For two entire months they had been searching for their pack mate, and now she was the lead they'd been waiting for. She glared back at that pit and steadied herself, pushing aside the panic and fear. Panic and fear would only make it more difficult to track down Korban, and apparently, Hati as well. She strode back over to the edge of the pit and peered down. Maybe there was some clue as to who had made this trap, and maybe that could lead to information as to where it came from— with a path they could track who was behind this.

The pit was deep and massive in size. It was also fairly old, with moss growing on some of the bricks down below. The bottom of the trap held a small pool of water that was speckled with larvae and tadpoles. Something metal glinted and caught her eye, a large metal hook that was welded onto a solid steel bar that seemed deeply embedded into the earth. Her eyes followed the edge of the pit and she noticed many more hooks along the rim. She walked alongside the edge of the hole, studying each hook carefully. They were dull, most of them painted over with some muddy brown color, probably to blend in and prevent rust. A few of the painted hooks were worn though, like the one she had spotted, and where the paint had been scraped off, the shiny metal gleamed through. Hooks that could have held a net.

"As hard as it has been raining, no wonder it's full of water down there," Odin murmured as he moved past her.

"This could be where your friend fell before," Sophie said after a moment of studying the deep puddle of water down below. She pointed and gestured to the large tadpoles darting around the pool. "See how they have fully developed legs, but they are still distinctly tadpoles as well? Not quite frogs yet. They're about eight weeks old."

Odin stared at her through his dark shades as she stood up again. Freki, who'd moved a little closer to inspect the area as well with the others, stared at her. "Not just brains... you're like Google smart. How the hell does someone like you know this random trivia crap?"

"I helped my son with his science project for school. It was on the life cycle of frogs." She smiled sadly. "It wasn't long before..." She trailed off, the memory of helping Danny with his drawings causing a lump to form in her throat. She could still smell the green crayon and saw his bright smile as they colored in the advanced doodles of her talented young son.

She would see him again. She would see Korban again.

She steeled herself and Val smiled to her. "I think I remember doing that project with my daughter too." She went over and put a comforting hand on Sophie's shoulder, which caused her to briefly tense, and then relax. "She's right. If this was the place that Hati was caught, we need to see what clues we can dig up. Any tracks may be pretty scarce, especially with all the rain and time that has passed. But any little clue may help us."

Val looked to Freki and Skoll. "I want the two of you to head back to camp, tell Geri what we have found. I want the three of you to stick together and see if you can find any more traps like this in the area. Mark the trail so you can all return here to let us know if you find anything," She gave them a meaningful look, "and be careful. I don't want whoever is setting these traps anywhere near our den, and I don't want to lose anyone else."

"You got it." Freki gave her a wink and a thumbs up then patted Skoll's arm. The poor guy still seemed shell-shocked from the whole thing, but he nodded and the pair headed into the woods.

Sophie watched as Freki pulled a switchblade out from his pocket and carved a delicate mark at about waist high into the bark of a tree nearby, then repeated the ritual as they headed deeper into the forest. As the pair vanished, Odin sighed heavily. "I don't like splitting up the pack, Val," he protested.

"I don't like it any more than you do," Val said with a frown. "We have to strike while the iron is hot. If someone is setting up these traps and able to hide away werewolves, there's something big and bad out here. For once it isn't just us wolves."

Odin nodded in agreement. "I bet the government is behind it," he murmured as he began to carefully search the grass for any more clues. "Who else could set up such well-made traps all the way the hell out here in the wilderness? It reeks of Feds."

To this, Val rolled her eyes and whispered to Sophie, "My husband has more conspiracy theories than the Illuminati have vowels." They joined in his search of the area for any sort of tracks embedded in the green grass. "Still, I do wonder who made these traps all the way out here. And what purpose they serve."

Sophie nodded in response. "I wonder who's behind this trap as well." It wasn't much to go on, but at least it was a start. She sighed and said, "So I guess we start here at square one."

"Yeah, any more evidence we find could help us. Footprints, scraps of cloth, or anything like that would be a good clue for when we finally do get our senses back," Val said as they walked carefully around the scene. "Even something old may provide a hint that Hati or Korban were here."

At mention of his name, Sophie's heart seemed to clench in response. She could hear his voice as she carefully searched for clues.

I love you.

Another lump formed in her throat, this one even harder to swallow down. She hadn't told him those three words back. And now... *not now.* She clenched her hand into a fist, her fingernails dug into her palm. *Focus. Concentrate.* She turned to Val. "I'm sorry for your missing pack member," she paused, then asked, "If you don't mind my asking, what brought you guys out here in the first place?"

"We came up here a couple months ago, and we were just passing through as we always do. Usually we stay the night along the lake, go through the Change, and then we go back to the open road. We have since we were infected." There she paused, but it wasn't a dramatic story telling effect. It was like she was having a moment of silence for their pack mates. She continued, "When we woke up the next morning, Hati was gone. We've been here looking for him since, and until now haven't had much luck finding any clues. Actually... until you told us what you saw last night, we weren't even certain if maybe he had become Wolven and ran away or something like that."

"No," Odin interrupted sternly, worriedly. "It isn't like Hati to run off. You know that."

"I know, honey," Valkyrie said diplomatically, "I'm just explaining to Sophie what we know." She turned back to Sophie. "Like Odin said, it isn't like him to run off. We've known each other forever, we've put many miles behind us together. But even before we became werewolves, we were a pack. We don't leave anyone behind on the road, and we won't here either. Until we ran into you this morning, we didn't have any idea what could have happened to him. But now that we know there are traps in the forest, and he's been missing..." She trailed off and Sophie nodded grimly, the butterflies suddenly worse in her stomach.

If she had any hope of Korban waiting for her at the trailer, it was now gone. She wouldn't be spending tonight laughing this off with him as some silly trap gone wrong. Something was definitely going on here if two werewolves were missing, one for a couple months now. How long would it be until she was able to have her Mate in her arms again?

She resumed her careful search and tried to reign in her emotions as a more powerful question bubbled into her mind.

When would she be able to tell him those three words back?

9: INHUMAN

Hours passed, or so it seemed, and no one had come to the room. Not the two bumbling idiots in camouflage or their boss. At least he thought hours passed. With no way of telling time, it was difficult to say. After some time though, he settled down and sat in the center of his cage. He wasn't going to risk burning his hands again, not with the chance they'd come back. He wanted to save his strength for when they showed themselves again.

Knowing there were others in this same situation in this very room, and yet how quiet, was also very unnerving. Aside from the breathing, and heavy breathing in one of the cages, they weren't saying a word. They hadn't even spoken up when those two idiots were there. "What is going on here? Why are you all just laying down and taking this?" Korban asked finally, and the response was pretty unanimous, hisses and shushing quietly erupting through the room.

"Keep it down, or they'll come back!" One of the voices warned.

Korban looked in the direction of the voice and growled, "I hope they do!"

"Idiot," one of the others said gruffly, his voice a growling whisper. "You think there is much we can do, given the situation? We're behind bars and they have weapons. Some of us are lucky to even have a scrap of clothing on us."

He had them talking. This was good. Maybe he could find out what was going on. And then... he wasn't sure what after that, but he'd come up with something. There had to be a way out of here.

Unless it was like that other place...

Keep them talking. He had to keep them talking. Quieter, he asked, "What is going on? Why are they putting us in cages?"

"You heard him, yeah? We're monsters to them," the man in the cage next to him with a weary British accent said softly.

"Yeah, pretty much." The angry, growling one spoke, and he could hear him shift in the darkness. "Monsters who bring them in money. Or some kind of other sick satisfaction."

Money? A billion options suddenly struck him, everything from sort of illegal slave trade to some sort of freak show where they were the showcase. "What do you mean, 'bring them in money?' What is going on here?" He felt like he was repeating himself, and he couldn't hide the panic in his voice at that moment.

"Don't get your panties in a twist. Oh right... no underwear. Nothing for it to go under." The growly man grumbled, and then explained. "You ever see the movie *Bloodsport*? Or *Fight Club*?"

"Yeah," Korban said.

"Well, so has this guy. Probably seen it a bit too much, because it gave him this idea. We aren't staying at some health club, but that much you can probably guess. They capture us and stuff us in cages, and force us to fight each other while they film it."

"Fight... each other...?" Korban repeated softly, almost wishing he hadn't, but he couldn't stop himself. He was simply in shock, the idea too horrifying to be real.

"Yes," the man said with much impatience, growling softly. "We fight, to the death. The winners get prizes, nothing extravagant but a scrap of clothing here, a decent steak for dinner. We're no better than dogs to them, waiting for the next match."

The thought made him sick to his stomach. "No... I won't do it. I won't fight."

"Heh. You say that now. They don't give you an option, buddy," any impatience was gone from his voice, replaced by sadness instead. "If you don't fight, they shoot your opponent first, then you."

An icy chill suddenly ran through him. He was naked, but this cold feeling went much deeper than that. It was one thing to stick his neck out and face the consequences. But to have someone else's blood on your hands...

"We all fight come the full moon. But they want a way to make the fights more constant. They've been working on something. Dragged the fella who was in your cage out a couple nights ago, and he didn't fight last night. I don't know what they did to him." The growling man was suddenly not so growly, in place of his anger there seemed to be a deep ache. "There were two others, too... but... he made us fight them..." He trailed off, unable to finish the horrible revelation.

This was getting worse and worse. This was such a violation of human rights, Korban didn't know where to begin.

"And we stay quiet for a reason. Don't expect them to bring you food or water tonight. If we make too much noise, they weaken us so that we don't have the strength to disobey." It sounded like the man flopped down again, or Korban believed he did. The darkness loomed a deeper black all of a sudden, or maybe it was the mood.

"So keep your mouth shut and just do what you're told. Maybe if you win enough bouts you'll get out of this place."

Korban sank down. He'd thought there was no worse place than that laboratory, with all the poking and prodding and constant supervision and testing, being treated more like a lab rat than a human being.

He was wrong.

~*~

It was starting to get dark when they finally stopped going over and over the area, with not much success in locating clues. Odin had spotted some indentations that looked like possible tire tracks, though the trail went cold when they reached the edge of the clearing and the path had been washed away from the rain. He marked the area as a point of reference for tracking later on when they searched the nearby area with the others. As the sun began to draw closer to the mountainous horizon, however, Val looked to Odin and the two exchanged a glance, before Val turned and said, "We should start heading back to the den. You should come with us. We need to stick together, especially if someone out there seems to be hunting wolves."

"I wouldn't even know where to begin to head back to where we were staying, anyway," Sophie shook her head and sighed. She didn't want to stop searching, but in the dark it was possible they could stumble into another one of these traps accidentally. "Maybe we'll spot something helpful on the way back, or maybe the guys had some luck finding another trap out there." Or better yet, they found Korban or their friend, or perhaps by some miracle, both.

Val nodded, a trace of a smile curving her lips as they turned and headed back into the forest together. Sophie watched as Odin took Val's hand and couldn't help but think of Korban. He was out there somewhere, and they would find him somehow, someway. She held onto that belief with all her heart. Hope was once again all she had left, and she clung to it.

They walked some distance from the clearing, and as they seemed to retrace their steps, the path changed, and it was then she noticed the distinct markings they had carved into the trees. Like some code, though they were slightly different from the ones that Freki had demonstrated earlier that day. They followed the winding path down to another clearing, only this time it was occupied by a large RV, a small trailer attached to a pickup truck, and a half dozen motorcycles. A small bonfire crackled as Freki, Skoll, and a man who looked like an older version of Freki, the same pale green eyes as his brother and a distinctive goatee that set the pair apart, along with a few smile lines that were etched into the older brother's face. "Geri, anything to report?" Odin asked as they approached the campsite.

The older version of Freki stood up, a frown emphasized by his dark goatee, though he did a double take when he saw Sophie. "Well, damn, I guess I owe you a drink next time we hit a bar, little brother," he stared at her, and then gazed to Odin. "Nothing found today, but Freki told me you guys found a lot. Including our missing celebrity. I can't believe we found Sophie Bane but haven't a damn clue as to where Hati ended up. That's our fucking luck."

"Language," Val growled. "Not in front of the kids."

As if on cue, the side door to the RV suddenly burst open and two young children, a girl who looked to be around Daniel's age and a smaller boy leapt and bound from the small set of steps and rushed toward Val and Odin. "Mommy! Daddy! You're home!"

Sophie froze. Watched as the two young, human offspring bounced toward their parents. Watched as both Val and Odin scooped up their children and held them. Watched smiles break out and relief fill the air. No fear, no panic. She didn't realize that she had been holding her breath until she exhaled, and then carefully inhaled, afraid of what she would do when their scent filled her nostrils again.

But nothing happened. The air here was full of the foreign wolf pack's scent. The children were human but they smelled like pack too. It was all so strange, so wonderful. A new hope filled her in that moment. "You... you have children?"

Val turned and nodded as she hugged her daughter close. They were a perfectly matched set, the four of them standing there. Blond and happy. "We have three children. This is Haley, and Connor," she gestured to her daughter then son respectively. "And our oldest, Evelyn, helps babysit on full moon nights. She's probably on her phone or computer inside."

Sophie smiled despite herself. "No Norse names for them?"

Val laughed. "We sort of adopted our biker names when we were bitten. We live off the grid and aren't the same people we were before. So there's no point in going by our old names anymore."

"So no one here has a human sponsor?" Sophie inquired.

"No, not exactly," Val kissed the top of her daughter's head as she held her close. "You know the rules. They would have taken our kids away. I wasn't about to let that happen, and neither was Odin. We keep them locked up in the RV during the full moon and we stay far away when we are wolves to keep them safe. Though with Hati gone missing, we have kept one of us behind to patrol and protect the den here, in case... well, we don't really know who we are dealing with here yet, now do we?" She patted Haley and then pecked Connor on the cheek. "Why don't you two go inside and brush your teeth, get your jammies on, and get ready for bed. I'll be in there in a moment to tuck you in and read you a story."

They groaned and protested, but a stern look from Valkyrie and they marched back into the RV as they were told.

"You… you don't feel any urge to attack your kids?" Sophie asked after a moment.

Val gave her an odd look, something between shock and disgust. "Of course not!" she snorted, then it seemed to dawn on her, and her expression softened. "Oh… of course. They tell everyone that, don't they. That's why they have those rules and laws in place, supposedly to protect the children from infection. I would never bite or hurt my kids. Neither would any of the guys here. They're safest with family. I won't let them fall into a system that is bullshit. They're my kids. My wolf even knows it. They're not prey. They're pack."

The words sunk in and Sophie felt a huge weight lift from her shoulders, a deep pain suddenly relieved after so long. It made sense. She wouldn't try to attack her own son. She couldn't wait to share the news with Korban that she would be safe around her son, that she wouldn't try to attack him like she had with Alex… and just like that, though the spark of hope remained, the pain returned. It must have shown on her face because Valkyrie murmured something to Odin who nodded and went into the RV after their children.

"I'll get you some clothes that may fit a bit better and we'll get a tent set up for you tonight. Try to rest. We'll have a long day ahead of us tomorrow. We won't stop until we find Hati. Or Korban for that matter." She headed up into the RV after her husband.

Sophie turned away, went over and sat on one of the gathered lawn chairs and stared into the fire. Freki came over, and she was about to give him hell, her eyes narrowed and ready to cuss him out if he so much as attempted to hit on her right now.

Her look must have been a real nasty one, as he gave a low whistle and extended his hand out carefully, offering a beer bottle to her, the cap still in place. "I come in peace," he said, cracking a nervous smile. "This is me, trying to apologize for being an ass earlier." He paused, then added, "Please don't hurt me."

Despite her sour mood, she forced a smile, but not before she made him squirm a little and made him wait a long, tense moment. She finally accepted the bottle, and he breathed a sigh of relief, pulled out his Swiss Army knife and popped the cap off her bottle. She wasn't a fan of beer, truth be told, but it was cold and maybe the alcohol would numb the pain for a little while. Freki sat in a chair beside her, careful not to move in too close. He cleared his throat. "I'm sorry about before," he began, and when she glanced to him without a glare he continued on. "I didn't realize you had lost someone important, too. I shouldn't have joked about it. My brother, hell, anyone in the pack will tell you I, uh, sometimes don't think things through. I should have just kept my mouth shut. I—"

Sophie held up her hand and swallowed a bitter but cold mouthful of beer. Then she said, "I accept your apology." She gazed back to the fire, and took another swig from the bottle. "Beer isn't enough though. You don't realize how important Korban is to me. He helped me when no one else could. He saved my life. He saved my humanity. You owe me more than a beer."

Freki swore under his breath, then stared at her. "More than a beer? How can I make it right then?"

She turned to him again. "You promise me, here and now, to do two things. One, please respect me. I'm okay with a flirty joke once in a while, but don't push your luck. And two…" She trailed off to hold him in suspense again, and then raised her beer to toast him. "You promise me that you will help me find Korban, and I promise you I will help you find Hati."

Freki clinked his bottle with hers and nodded in agreement. "Fair enough. All right then, Sophie. You got yourself a promise."

She smiled and they downed the rest of their drinks.

~*~

76

There was the hum of electricity, and then the lights clicked on and blinded everyone in the room once again. Korban had dozed off in a fitful sleep, but quickly jumped, sat up, and rubbed his eyes. He wasn't sure how long he slept. The smell of charred, greasy beef wafted into the air, and a squeaky cart was pushed in by the two camouflage-covered men. Korban's stomach growled. How long had it been since he'd last eaten? Usually after the full moon he was ravenous, but given the fact that his mind had been occupied by everything else going on, he hadn't given much thought to food until that moment.

The pair of men paused in front of each cage and dropped a paper plate with ground beef to the ground, and then shoved the plate into the crate through a shallow opening that Korban hadn't noticed before at the bottom of their prisons. It resembled dog food, but his empty stomach didn't care. They went around and dropped off paper plates of overcooked meat and plastic bottles filled with water. They were careful not to get too close to any of the cages, silver bars or not. The large one muttered as he served the food. "Feeds these mongrels better than us sometimes, I swear."

The smaller one only laughed at that. "Right." He dropped a plate in front of the cage that held the growling man, who quietly glowered at their captors but remained thin-lipped and silent, even when he eagerly grabbed at the bottle and the plate and began to devour handfuls of the ground meat.

They paused in front of Korban's cage, the small one's eyes lit with amusement as he stared at him through the mask. "Hungry, Mouth?" He snickered.

Korban growled as his eyes dangerously narrowed. He was famished and thirsty, but if it meant groveling for this man to give him a meal, he had another thing coming. "Not if it means kissing your ass," Korban snapped.

The larger guard laughed at that, and the other's eyes narrowed. "Smart mouth, I see. We'll see how snappy you are after skipping a meal or two."

"I wouldn't eat anything you offered me anyway." Korban glared defiantly, too angry to let his growling stomach override his thoughts. "For all I know it's been poisoned."

Now the scrawny one laughed. "Ah, if only we could. I would so enjoy that. But I'm afraid we don't provide an easy way out. Especially not for someone like you, Mouth."

Korban's lip curled at that. "Go to hell."

"After you, mongrel." The little one snarled back then placed the plate down for the man in the cage beside him, kicking the paper plate toward him and knocking some of the meat onto the floor of the British man's cage.

They ignored Korban and finished handing out the meat and water, then left the room, leaving the lights on for now. The moment the door closed his stomach rumbled again in protest, but he was still too angry and stubborn to plead to those men for anything. He paced in his cage, doing his best to ignore the others as they chewed and slurped.

The man beside him stared at his plate and rubbed his temples. Then with a defeated look he not only ate the offered food on his plate, but the precious morsels that had scattered on the floor of his cage as well.

"They call us monsters, but they are the ones treating us like animals." Korban muttered softly. He wouldn't starve to death in one night, but it was becoming more difficult to think with his newly roused hunger and thirst.

"Assholes... both of them," the growling man grumbled, then

folded and shoved the empty paper plate through his crate so hard it ended up sliding across to Korban's crate, an inch of it making it into the slot.

To Korban's surprise, there was a small handful of ground beef on what he had assumed was an empty plate. He gazed over in wonder at the other man who just smirked. "Just because they don't feed you, doesn't mean I won't try."

"Thank you. Really," Korban gratefully accepted the left overs and though his hands shook a little, forced himself to eat what little food the man had given him slowly. He savored each nibble of the plain, charred beef. "I'm Korban, Korban Diego," he introduced himself, and then spontaneously added, "Friends call me Lobo."

The blond haired man across from him with the collection of sun and moon-themed tattoos on his arms, grinned. "Friends call me Hati."

"I'm Spike," the man with the blanket piped in after he paused licking his plate clean.

Korban's gaze turned to the British man, who seemed even more wearied after finishing their meager meal. He didn't say anything for a long moment, then sighed and quietly added. "If you need a name, call me Blaze. That's all you need to know."

"You're a British werewolf," Korban commented.

"Right," Blaze muttered dryly, sniffed and frowned. "Imagine my astonishment when I realized that this bloody virus could be spread to any human, regardless of their homeland."

"How did you end up here in New York?" Korban asked.

"That's a long story, mate," Blaze said flatly and glanced to the double doors across the way. "They'll be back any moment. Get to the point."

"You'll have to forgive Blaze, he's been here the longest as far as I gather," Hati supplied grimly. "I've been maybe two months now but you catch on to their rules quick."

"What is the point anyway?" Spike interjected in a defeated tone. "Those maniacs out there are going to make us fight each other to the death. He's already made us do it before. I don't want to feel worse than I already do, getting to know you guys. Especially Blaze." He glared over at the British werewolf.

His body language gave his true feeling away though as Blaze turned his attention to Spike and the man flinched. "Do you think I like being their reigning champ? Do you think I like being here the longest? Watching these cages empty and fill again?" Blaze growled and Spike cowered further back in his cage.

"N-no," Spike stammered, and though he appeared larger than Blaze, taking up more space in his cage, he still shrunk himself as much as possible away from the man. Even though his cage wasn't close to his.

Blaze's glare softened, but before he could say anything more the double doors burst open again. Korban scrambled to kick the paper plate out of his crate to hide the evidence but it was too late. The scrawny man frowned as they strode over to the cages. The large man gripped a trash bag while he wielded a long, pointed metal stick.

The drill sergeant frowned at the paper plate outside of Korban's crate. "Making friends, Mouth? That's a very stupid idea here. An idea like that will get you killed." He loomed near Korban's cage but was careful not to get too close as he taunted him. "Of course, I will enjoy scraping your corpse up from the ring."

Something about the way he said it so casually sent a chill through Korban. The smaller man scowled and stabbed the stick into the empty plates on the ground and stuffed them in the bag that his partner was holding open. "Davey's already gonna be pissed at us for not watchin' 'em eat. Don't get 'em riled up now too. You know he likes it when they're hungry."

The hulking man glanced around as his comrade finished picking up the trash and scoffed. He glared at Korban before he turned his attention to Hati. "You got something to say, Mongrel? You got lucky the other night. You may not be so lucky in your next match." Hati glared defiantly back at him, squared his jaw, but said nothing. The masked captor continued. "Maybe if you aren't feelin' as hungry, willin' to defy the rules still, maybe you need a reminder of who's in charge here. I think a few days without food for both of you will smarten you up." As if to bring his point home he snarled at Spike and Blaze as well. "You think it's some kind of summer camp we're runnin' here? Here's a reminder for all of ya'll. You aren't friends, you are monsters, and you'll be only makin' it worse if you decide to get soft here. Don't talk to each other. Don't bother makin' friends. You'll be at each other's throats soon enough like the beasts you are. So to remind ya'll of that... I think tomorrow Jimmy and I will forget to bring your meals and water. We got plans anyway, don't we?"

The scrawny man – Jimmy – nodded and pointed at Korban with the stick. "This one may not know better, but I thought the Mongrel would. I guess after a day we'll find out."

The drill sergeant only smirked darkly and Korban hated him more as he gloated. "I guess we will, won't we? Better ration that water you have boys, that's all you're gettin' and tomorrow is supposed to be a hot one." He paused and sneered down at Korban. "Oh. Looks like someone doesn't have any, does he? What? Nothing to say now? And here I thought you were stupid. Pretty smart to keep your mouth shut now. Save your spit because you're gonna need it with two days without food or water."

Rage rose inside of him and Korban saw red. He lunged forward but remembered the silver and stopped himself, which evoked a laugh from drill sergeant. He spit at the man's feet, who grabbed the metal stick from Jimmy and swatted the edge of Korban's cage. Korban flinched backward and he laughed. "Just for that, Mouth, it'll be three days now." He snapped the trash bag closed and gestured to Jimmy. "Let's go."

Three days? Though his stomach growled he glared as their captors once again headed out from the room. Spike whimpered as he held up his half-empty water bottle, but didn't say anything more. Blaze glared at Korban but didn't say a word. The only one who didn't blame Korban with a look was Hati, who clenched his jaw and fists as he watched Jimmy and the drill sergeant slam the doors behind them. The lights went out and silence reigned again.

"I'm sorry," Korban blurted, to which came the return of nothing but being hissed and shushed into silence. This time, Korban wisely obeyed, though inside he reeled.

More questions came to mind, questions he wanted to ask his fellow prisoners but there was no way they'd talk to him now. Who was Davey? Was he the one he'd dubbed the drill sergeant, or somebody else? What about this Pit he had mentioned before? The silence and darkness that surrounded them seemed more menacing than before. His empty stomach rumbled again and he laid down on the ground, facing the direction of the double doors.

He missed his friends and home, but more than anything he missed Sophie. At least she had not been caught in that net with him and wasn't stuck in this horrible place. Wherever she was, he prayed she was safe.

10: SEARCH

The next morning Sophie woke up early. The sky was still dark but the stars were starting to fade into the break of day. The air was damp and chilly but her sleeping bag was dry and warm. She stretched and yawned, blinking. For the briefest moment she was at peace, in that place between sleep and awake where she was still with Korban, the sleeping bag was Korban's arms around her, and he was snuggled against her, safe and sound. When she blinked again, the sleeping bag was the only thing there and she sighed in disappointment. She closed her eyes again and took in a few deep breaths. She could smell another wolf on this sleeping bag, and wondered if it was their missing pack mate's. The thought was depressing.

She would help them find their friend, and hoped that this would be the same path to find Korban. If not... maybe if they found their pack mate, they would help her find Korban in turn. She hoped where ever he was, he was safe, and that he had something soft and warm around him.

There was snoring, but she could pick up the sounds of the waking forest around her too. The delicate steps of a deer, the whistle of a light breeze through the leaves and grass, and the chirping of an early bird. She could smell the moss and the maples and evergreens, damp with morning dew. Inhaling it deeply, she tried to pick up any other scent, any hint that maybe Korban was nearby. She had no such luck.

Sighing, she got up, feeling too restless to stay down any longer. She paced quietly along the edge of the camp. Every moment that passed, Korban might be farther and farther away. Luckily, the others started to wake, as if also just as anxious to begin their search. She rolled up her sleeping bag up and stoked the smoldering ashes that remained for the fire, adding some dry branches and twigs to it to get it rekindled again. She had a good little fire going by the time everyone was awake. Freki lifted both eyebrows in surprise when he emerged from his tent and saw her handiwork. "Good morning, Sophie. You aren't just some city girl after all, are you?"

Sophie smiled. "You bet your ass I'm not just some sheltered city girl."

Geri's hearty chuckle came as he followed his brother out of the tent. "Good. Do you mind grabbing some more kindling and I'll put breakfast on? We have eggs and some bacon."

She needed a distraction until they were on the move again. As much as she itched to run and search for Korban, it wouldn't be wise to blindly search for him. She nodded to Geri. "Sure."

"I'll help," Freki offered and she nodded again.

"Don't go too far, we're going to eat and get back to the hunt as soon as we can," Geri cautioned as they walked away from the camp.

They gathered fallen sticks from nearby until the smell of eggs and bacon wafted in their direction and summoned them back to camp. The night before Valkyrie offered some food after giving her a fresh set of clothes, but she hadn't had much of an appetite despite not eating that day. Her stomach was empty but so was her heart. This morning, however, it seemed her hunger returned. She needed her strength to find Korban.

They gathered up around the campfire and Geri served up scrambled eggs and bacon on paper plates. Freki sat beside her, while Odin, Val, and Skoll sat across from her. Val's three children had sleepily emerged for breakfast at her call, the two little ones sat on Odin and Skoll's laps, while Val's older daughter, Evelyn, sat close to her mother and stared wide-eyed at Sophie from across the fire. She had a short, stylish hair cut that was dyed black— the signature blonde roots of her family were just beginning to break free at the base of her scalp. "You're that missing billionaire's wife," she gawked, and her mother gave her a look. "What? She is. Like, everyone was looking for you. But they had your funeral and buried you. I saw it online during a live stream. Are you not just a werewolf but like, a zombie too?"

"Forgive my Evelyn's manners, she's seventeen and thinks she knows best," Val apologized.

"Seventeen and a half, Mom, and please call me Evie," Evelyn corrected, then blushed and smiled sheepishly. "Sorry, I don't mean to offend you. I never met a celebrity before."

Sophie only smiled and shook her head. "It's okay. I'm sort of used to it by now," she turned to Evie. "I'm just a werewolf, like your parents and their pack. I promise I'm not the walking dead."

"Well, Evie, you'll be grounded until you're eighteen and a half if you continue to stare and be rude to our guest," Val chided.

Odin cleared his throat and diverted their attention. "I think maybe we should plan out our manhunt so we can get right to it," he gazed around at his remaining pack. "If what we have found and what I suspect is true, Hati – and Korban – are in trouble. I also think, based on what we know so far, that there may be other traps like that one out in the woods. I know what I said before, but we can cover more ground if we split into groups. However… I think we need to use the good ol' fashioned buddy system here. No one goes out into the forest alone. We should check in at a certain time to make sure partners don't get lost either."

Geri nodded. "Want us to start at that pit from yesterday?"

Odin finished his food on his plate and pulled out a folded paper map. He pointed to a small red rectangle he'd placed not far from where he'd put an X labelled "The Den." "We scoured that area yesterday, I don't think we'll find much there, but we may revisit it tomorrow. Right now we need to focus on my theory. If there are other traps, this could be set up by someone professional. Someone with the means to afford such advanced wolf pits and removable nets. Someone who knows the area but has the money to invest in… who knows what."

Geri growled, "The government."

Val frowned but didn't say anything, and Evie rolled her eyes. "Let's focus on a plan, not a theory right now, darlin'," Val said, and looked over to Sophie. "Freki failed to mention with all his antics yesterday that he has one hell of a sniffer. If Hati was only gone for a few days, and he was caught in that trap, he would have been able to trail him if he had so much as a whiff of his scent. Unfortunately it's been so long now, he wouldn't be able to track Hati by scent. But if we can find the trap that Korban was recently in, maybe we can still track him down and find out if he ended up where Hati is as well. Where were the two of you staying?"

"We found an abandoned trailer and made our camp there." Hope swelled up inside of her again. "If we found it again, Korban's scent could be there, or if by some chance he was able to get out of the trap maybe he would be there, or around there looking for me."

"If you got me something with his scent on it, or if we found another trap, it could be a good lead to go on," Freki agreed. "And it would be even better if he was there waiting, then we'd have someone else to help find Hati."

Odin nodded, scratched his blond beard on his chin. "All right then. We'll break into three groups. Group one will be Geri and me, we will go search for any more traps in the area. Group two will be Val, Sophie, and you Freki… you'll go together and see if you can locate that trailer. Skoll, you will stay here as part of group three and make sure no one else comes to camp… or leaves it." He gave a pointed look to Evie with that, though his gaze roamed over to his little ones too. "Right now it's not safe to go into the woods. You three mind your Uncle Skoll. Someone is out there laying traps for werewolves but who knows what their intentions really are. Please do not argue with me on this, Evie. You and Skoll need to stay here and look out for your brother and sister, and yourselves."

Evie nodded, though Skoll looked hurt. "I want to help find my brother, Odin, please—"

"Do not argue with Odin, Skoll," Val stated firmly. "We need to hold it together in order to find your brother. Don't go rogue on us now. We have a plan, let's stick to it. We will find Hati faster if we do this the smart way." She finished her breakfast and tossed the paper plate into the fire. "Let's get moving."

They nodded, and quickly finished breakfast. Sophie turned away as Val and Odin said their goodbyes to their family, tossed her own empty plate into the fire, and watched it burn.

We're coming, Korban, she thought to herself as the others got ready. She prayed that they would find him back at the trailer, smiling that Cheshire-cat grin of his and looking relieved that she was also safe and sound.

~*~

Korban woke up after another fitful nap and wondered why he even bothered trying to sleep. It seemed every time he tried to doze off it only made him more exhausted to wake up cold, hungry, naked, and alone. He wondered what Sophie was doing now. She must be looking for him, worried sick, and sadly with good reason. But on the off chance that maybe she'd been captured too...

No. She would be in this room, wouldn't she? He'd be even more enraged to have her exposed to those two bumbling idiot guards, whoever this Davey was, and all these other wolves. Silver or not, he wouldn't let those bars stand between him and Sophie. He contemplated the chance to escape. If he could stand it, he could bend those bars, he was sure of it. Once he'd regained his strength he easily could, burning sensation or not.

The thoughts that remained with him while he was awake were no different than his nightmares. Visions of being forced to murder another man, to have to face another werewolf... He kept replaying many clips from his own life in his mind. A stupid school yard fight when he was younger. Only this time instead of facing the school yard bully who picked on RJ, it was with the massive black wolf, who moved so fast he only saw the blur of dark fur, a flash of bright silver glinting as he pounced. His scar along his collar stung with the memory of those sharp teeth that sealed his fate.

He could see the doctors then, the men and women in their surgical masks who hovered around him, poking and prodding him, and the injections of drugs that wore off all too quickly. Until finally Alex and RJ, along with Pops, were hovering over him, calling his name, bringing him back from the hell he'd gone through.

It was so different, those white and bright, clean walls compared to this dark, cramped prison. And yet, the feelings were the same. He felt trapped and for a moment he couldn't breathe. His eyes flickered in the darkness, tried to find the exit. One of the others snorted in his sleep, and he glanced into the opposite direction... somewhere over there in the inky blackness he was sure he could see the shadow of a door.

Suddenly the wolf was stirring inside him. Even though the full moon had just passed he could almost feel the fur brush beneath his skin. Waking up early, pissed off that his Mate was not near, that he was stuck in a cage, he was starving and unable to escape. There was danger, and the wolf was trying to take over, to defend himself where the human side had failed. But shifting here and now, to lose control, that would mean putting the other prisoners here in danger, or worse, he would be in danger of losing himself completely, and become nothing but a mindless and bloodthirsty Wolven. Which would be perfect for their sick form of entertainment, their own personal werewolf *Fight Club*.

He closed his eyes and tried to calm himself down. He wished he could talk with the others, and maybe together they could figure a way out of there. He'd caused enough pain for them already and it was only his first day there, as far as he could tell. Another opportunity would come up, and maybe then they could work together and find a way out of this. He felt dizzy and weak, usually after a full moon he'd wake up safe in the garage, RJ would have coffee and breakfast going, the smell of it divine in his memory, and he felt his mouth water. His stomach grumbled once more in protest.

He ignored his hunger and thirst as best as he could, and tried to focus on good things waiting back home. He thought of RJ and Alex, and most of all, Sophie. She had to be safe out there. She was many things, but helpless was not one of them. He'd come to realize that since he first met her. She wasn't some damsel in distress, even when he rescued her from a vicious Wolven she had proven to be much more than that.

If there was anyone out there who could save him, save them all, it was Sophie. As long as there was hope he wouldn't fall into the darkness. He clung to that thread with all he could. His sanity and life depended on it.

~*~

Once again they were searching through the forest, but this time Sophie was more alert. The first time she'd woken on two legs the forest all appeared to be the same to her eyes. Now there were subtle differences as they wandered along a familiar path, a patch of flowers here and a bit of moss there— things that made certain areas stand out. They kept their conversations short but pleasant, and quiet. Just in case they missed out on an unusual noise, or audible clue that would lead them to their missing pack mates.

Sophie glanced up at the sky through the trees. White, fluffy patches of cloud floated high above them, bright against the pale blue. She would cross her fingers every once in a while. Korban had a stronger memory of being a wolf. Maybe when they found him they could get even more clues to find Hati for his pack.

The path split up ahead and she stopped. "I think... the trailer may be this way," she said. She thought she recognized the way and once again wished she could remember more from when she was a wolf.

Freki moved forward, sniffed the air and nodded. "You have good instincts; I can smell your scent in that direction."

Sophie tilted her head a little and asked, "You can track my scent, but you haven't been able to get a hint of Korban yet?"

"I can track scents I am familiar with, people and wolves I have met," he confessed a bit sheepishly. "But to be honest without something with Korban's scent I may not be able to track him directly, werewolf or not. This forest is already teeming with scents, and believe it or not, there are actually a lot of strange werewolf scents around the area."

"So there are other werewolves out here in the Adirondacks? Right now?" Sophie shouldn't have been so surprised, but it had seemed like her and Korban were the only two werewolves out here in the wilderness until she'd run into Val and Odin's pack.

"Yeah, it's kind of crazy how many of us are out here at the moment." Freki led the way as they started down the path to the left. "Lots of people like us are up here, especially this time of year. Wide open spaces, plenty of critters to hunt, and only a few humans before the real camping season opens. We heard it was safe and quiet up here from another werewolf, and we were passing through anyway, so we decided to camp and check it out. It was everything he said it was, until the full moon when Hati disappeared."

"How long were you guys here before he vanished?" Sophie asked as they walked along.

"We'd been here two weeks before he went missing," Val piped up. "Not too long after the thaw. We only planned on staying until after the full moon. We don't stay in one place too long."

Of course they wouldn't, and Sophie knew and understood why. Valkyrie and Odin had three important reasons to avoid quarantine back at the den. The longer they could avoid being caught, the better.

A breeze brushed by them from up ahead and Sophie froze. Between the scent of flora and fauna she caught his distinct musk and her heart skipped a beat. "Korban," she breathed out his name.

She rushed ahead, her own human nose working as hard as it could. Freki and Val flanked her, followed her as his scent grew closer. Her heart raced as the smell grew stronger, and she sprinted toward him. "Korban!" She called out to him again, feeling as though she would burst at the sight of him as she rounded the corner where his scent seemed to be coming from.

The tiny clearing opened before her, empty, and her heart sank. She saw it there, right where they had left it— the bag with her and Korban's clothing for after the full moon. His scent was faded from the clearing itself, but when she went over to where he'd hung the borrowed clothes, his strong scent filled her nostrils. She approached the bag slowly. If Korban hadn't found his way back here… was he really lost, like Hati? Maybe somehow he'd ended up finding the trailer, or went there to try and find Sophie first.

She pulled the bag down and cradled it close to her chest, breathed in his scent. She jumped when Val gently clapped a hand on her shoulder. "That should help us find him," Valkyrie said as she offered a smile.

"Oh yeah, that will work," Freki said. "We'll find your trailer in no time, and who knows? Maybe we'll at least have one reunion to celebrate tonight."

Sophie fought back the urge to howl in sorrow and frustration. She managed to swallow the lump in her throat, "Let's keep going then."

"Yeah, we should keep tracking for as long as we can before the rain hits," Valkyrie said, and pointed up to the sky.

Sophie turned her attention back up above them and saw the puffy clouds that had gathered had turned gray. She almost laughed. It was like nature had turned to match her mood. She reluctantly handed the bag to Freki when he held out his hand, and he held it up to his nose, took in a deep breath, and then exhaled slowly. He turned and gestured in another direction. "This way."

They followed him, and Sophie let him lead the way, suddenly very quiet. She couldn't get her hopes up again like that. She prayed she was wrong, but she couldn't fight the sinking feeling that Korban had remained in that trap… and hopefully the others would find him before something terrible happened to him.

11: MANHUNT

Korban wasn't at the trailer, and as their trail went cold and dark, clouds gathered above them and Val suggested they start heading back to the den. Defeated for now, Sophie agreed without much protest.

They gathered up some supplies, and Sophie collected the bag with their clothes from the night before the full moon. She left a note for Korban just in case he did show up here when they were gone. She wanted to leave directions to the den too, but Val seemed nervous. She wrote down in the letter how they would check in on the trailer until she found him, and that she was safe where she was for now. She added for him to stay put and wait for her, and almost signed it "Love," but stopped herself. She wanted to say it the first time out loud to him, not write it. She should have told him before. Even now her hand shook as she finished the message.

It wasn't much, but Sophie hoped he would get there and read the message. She felt drained and heartbroken. She wanted to keep searching. They had Korban's scent now, and she wanted to keep moving while the trail was fresh in the forest. There were always risks, but that shouldn't stop them. With every passing minute it seemed their chance to find him shrunk.

"We should get back and rendezvous with the others, maybe they found something," Val suggested, a sympathetic look in her wolf-like eyes. "I'm sorry we didn't find him here, but at least we have something to go on. Maybe if they've found another one of those traps, Freki will be able to pick up his scent."

They made it back to the campsite before the rain began to pour, and the final blow of the day was discovering that Odin and Geri hadn't found anything at all in their search.

"Unfortunately nothing to be found in the directions we picked today, but we'll pick up the search for more traps tomorrow," Odin tried to reassure everyone as the rain began to fall.

Sophie quietly retired for the night into her tent and no one stopped her. A solemn comradery fell around them as they each missed their lost pack mate, swallowing the bitter defeat of another day without many answers.

Sophie curled into her sleeping bag as the rain pelted the plastic covering of her tent. Korban was still out there, somewhere. She reached and opened up the bag of clothes, and took out one of his shirts she had packed. She drew the shirt close and buried her face into it, breathed in his scent of pine trees, male musk, and home.

Tears welled in her eyes as her emotions weighed heavy on her heart. She wanted to go out there, storm or not, and continue to search for him. Was he stuck in one of those traps in the rain? Was he hungry or hurt? "Where are you now, Korban?" she whispered out loud, and wished somehow she would know the answer.

~*~

To Korban's surprise when he woke he found himself tangled in a net, staring up at a clear, blue sky.

How he'd ended up here, he couldn't remember. The soft sounds of the waking forest filled the air. Had that horrible place been just a nightmare? It had been so vivid.

Cool air brushed against his bare, warm skin. He rubbed his eyes, sniffed the air. He caught a hint of mint and vanilla in the midst of the wild scent of forest. "Sophie?" he called to her.

She appeared above the trap and looked down at him with a smile. "There you are!" she laughed. "How'd you end up down there?"

He blushed. She was already dressed in their borrowed clothes and put a hand on her hip as she gazed down into the pit. "I... sort of stumbled upon it. Help me outta here?"

Sophie nodded, then leapt down into the net with a carefree laugh, rolling beside him as the net caught her too. Her arms slid around him and he was suddenly very okay to be stuck in the net as she straddled his body and gazed down upon him. "I've got you where I want you now."

Korban moaned, "Sophie..."

She bent down and her lips met his and for a blissful, long moment the world melted away. When she broke away he almost whimpered, and her finger rested on his lips. "Shh... quiet, they're coming."

"Sophie?" Korban inquired, and she put a finger to her lips.

"Shhh..."

His head began to hurt, and a low growl made him jump, then he realized it was his stomach. He opened his mouth to speak again and Sophie urgently shook her head at him. "They're here."

He was greeted again by darkness.

"Shit man, you even talk in your sleep? Shut up, they're here!" Hati hissed.

Korban groaned. The dream wasn't a nightmare, this place he'd ended up in was, and he already missed the peaceful, floating feeling and the memory of Sophie's kiss.

"Who's Sophie?" asked Spike in a hushed whisper, but the double doors opened once more, the lights clicked on and blinded them, and he went silent.

Three men walked in. The new stranger led the way, and though he was slightly shorter than drill sergeant he was built like him. Pure, lean muscle. He carried himself like he was in charge, and at the sudden cowering looks of Jimmy and his partner in crime, it seemed this was their ring leader.

His eyes adjusted on the leader, who wore a tan-colored tank top and camouflage pants, complete with black combat boots. He had short, shaggy brown hair with long bangs that shielded his eyes, and a rough looking goatee that circled and emphasized his grim frown. Unlike the other two, he didn't wear a ski mask to hide his identity. "Why didn't you tell me we had a new guest, Earl?"

Drill Sergeant flinched as if he'd been struck and quickly stammered, "It was after the full moon and we had it under control, you seemed exhausted so we handled it."

The ring leader stopped near Korban's cage. "Wasted a silver bullet I see. We'll have to move him."

"I'm sorry Davey, really," Earl swallowed anxiously. "It won't happen again. I swear it."

"It better not," Davey growled, then kneeled down so he was face to face with Korban.

Korban's eyes narrowed, but then widened in surprise. Davey's eyes also opened in amazement, and then a slow grin spread across his face. "Well look at that, boys," Davey's grin continued to widen, more menacing, like baring his teeth to snarl. "We caught something really special in our trap this time."

Korban's heart raced, threatened to burst from his chest. His dry mouth only seemed to get drier. Davey laughed, but the merriment of his voice never reached his eyes.

His yellow, wolf-like eyes that were frighteningly too familiar.

"What's your name, pal?" Davey asked, studying him over as he circled his crate.

"Korban Diego," he managed to croak in a weak voice. He tried to remain confident and strong but his empty stomach was beginning to take its toll.

"Korban Diego," Davey repeated, then smirked and licked his lips. "I'm David, David Bailey. Friends call me Davey. You know… we've been doin' this awhile but you're the first one I've seen with special eyes like mine. Has it always been this way for you too?"

He nodded and regretted the move as the room seemed to spin a little after. He grimaced as his stomach growled.

Davey chuckled. "Wow. Wowee." He frowned and turned to face Earl and Jimmy. "You two not bein' hospitable to our new guest? No food or water?"

"N-no sir, Davey, just like ye said, he's been dry since we checked in yesterday—" Earl began, but shrunk at the look Davey gave him.

His expression smoothed by the time he turned around. "Korban here is special. Go get some steaks on, rare, and bring him a beer. Hell, bring one for the whole group. We're goin' to party tonight, and get back to training tomorrow."

The two minions and the three other werewolves stared at Davey, expressions filled with surprise, curiosity, and a hint of mistrust. Davey merely smiled down at Korban. "We'll keep him strong, and ready to fight. I want him to be ready for the next battle. I expect that he will be one helluva opponent." He had a dreamy, starry-eyed look. "This will be… my greatest battle. Finally against a truly worthy werewolf. Someone just like me."

~*~

A cold chill woke her, something colder than the damp mountain air raced down her spine and her eyes flashed open as her body jolted awake. There was no hazy moment of bliss this morning, only the harsh reality that Korban was still gone, only made worse by the unshakable feeling that he was in danger. She neatly folded his shirt and tucked it back into the bag with the rest of his clothes before she rolled up the sleeping bag and headed out of the tent.

The campsite was quiet; it seemed she was the first one awake again this morning. The sky above was lightening up, and the rising sun still covered with a thick blanket of clouds. There was nothing she wanted to do more than to get out there and keep searching. The sooner they started, the sooner they would find them. Her stomach twisted with a nagging feeling that wouldn't go away. She whimpered under her breath and began to pace. No one else was awake yet, and as tempting as it was to go run off and try to search on her own, she knew it would be foolish to go off alone. If she ended up stuck in one of those wolf traps, she'd be no better off than she was now. Stuck, alone, and Korban still out there, somewhere, probably also stuck and alone.

This wasn't helping. This wasn't helping at all.

Frustrated, she went over to Freki's tent, which he shared with his brother. A duet of snoring greeted her as she approached. "Freki? Freki!" Sophie hissed. "Wake up!"

Freki groaned, "This is not the way I fantasize being woken up by a beautiful woman."

Sophie scowled, her patience already thin this morning. "What did I say about flirting with me? Get up and make yourself useful instead."

Geri's snores transformed into a low chuckle, and Freki sat up, his hair sticking out in every direction. "Okay, okay, sorry, I don't remember all the rules the moment I wake up." He rubbed his eyes and yawned. "Especially this early."

"We need to search before it starts raining again," Sophie insisted, that feeling inside of her urgent, and she swallowed down some of the panic that came with it. "Please."

Freki really looked to her then, nodded, and the jokes were set aside for now. "Okay. You got it. Give me a moment to get dressed and we'll get started."

"Thank you," Sophie stepped away so he could get dressed. She resumed her pacing, and started to pray that today would be different, and soon she would be reunited with her Mate.

Her Mate. The words were true in her heart, and yet she hadn't been able to tell him that she loved him. That lump returned in her throat but thankfully Freki was pretty quiet as they walked, yawning and stretching and listening to the forest that surrounded them.

She remembered one night, when she was alone with Korban back at their impromptu campsite. They were still tangled together, sprawled out on the grass-stained blankets after they made love. She could still hear his heartbeat as it pounded along with hers, amplified and steady as she laid her cheek against his chest. "I'm so lucky," she whispered to him as the stars blinked above them through thin threads of clouds. "Maybe it didn't seem that way at first... but if I hadn't met you that night... who knows what I would have become."

His fingers threaded through her hair and the feeling of his warm fingertips as they brushed her scalp was exquisite. "I know I'd be lost without you," Korban confessed.

"You, and RJ too, for that matter, would be in a whole lot less trouble if we didn't cross paths that night," she said, feeling a twist of guilt as she said it, and propped herself up on her elbows to look him in his eyes, which were the color of honey in the dim moonlight. "What makes you think you'd be lost without all the trouble I've brought into your lives? You nearly lost Alex, you lost your home, and you almost lost your humanity… all because of me."

His face scrunched up a little at that as he shook his head defiantly. Those honey orbs gazed up to her, filled with emotion as he frowned. "I don't see it that way," he said as his arms slid around her. "My life before you wasn't all that great. I was treading water, just to keep my head above it. I survived the attack, but I wasn't living my life. Not until you came into it."

Her heart gave a little flutter at his words. "It's still hard for me to imagine that no woman before me didn't see what I see in you," she caressed his cheek with her hand, eyes locked with his. "Wolf eyes or not. Werewolf or not. You are something special, Korban."

He smiled at her words though his cheeks darkened. "The dating game became a little more complicated after being bitten. Not too many people want to be with someone who has to be tethered to a sponsor for just about everything. It really doesn't impress others when you have to report to a chaperone every night. Or if there's a curfew in effect, and you have to be in earlier than Cinderella, or risk your life sneaking around to see a late movie. It would have cramped RJ's style, too, if he wasn't already with Alex. If you think dating as a single father is a challenge, try going on a date, and explaining you're the legal guardian of a werewolf." He paused and shook his head, smirked at the thought that crossed his mind before he shared it. "I really, really owe him many drinks when we get back home."

She had laughed, and then the quiet fell again between them as he held her and they admired one another without words.

I love you; he had said the words and meant it just days before. She opened her mouth in that sweet silence, steeled herself to return those words. He cupped the back of her head and drew her down for a kiss before a single sound emerged. Her heart was so full in that moment she leaned in as he guided her down.

Just the memory of his warm, sweet mouth against hers sent a rush of heat through her and renewed her determination to find him. The man she loved. Her Mate.

I'm coming Korban, we're coming to find you.

As much as his stomach was relieved to have food in it again, and his thirst sated after almost two days without something to drink, Korban remained uneasy the rest of the night, and into the early morning hours. Davey's words echoed in his mind and the mad look in his eyes haunted him. It was some kind of twisted joy that filled the other werewolf's golden eyes. They had left the lights on that night as Davey promised to return in the morning, "When the real training will begin," he had said, his grin remaining as they closed the doors.

Someone just like me.

The words made the steak and beer churn in his stomach. The others in their cages seemed to regard him differently now too. Blaze continued to scowl at him when they exchanged glances, but he now quickly averted his gaze, as though suddenly afraid to look into his eyes too long. Korban was used to the gawking stares back home, but somehow when these other werewolves did it, it stung like a fresh wound instead of an old one. Maybe it just reminded him a little too much of the familiar prejudices, and reopened feelings of being outcast, only worse because now it was by some who shared the same affliction as him.

Needless to say, despite his hunger being resolved, Korban couldn't sleep much that night, and the silence seemed even heavier, until finally that familiar metallic crack of the outer door's lock rang out like a shotgun blast and caused them to jump. Davey strode in, wearing a fresh set of green camo pants and his black combat boots, but foregoing a shirt today. His yellow eyes locked right on to Korban, causing his stomach to lurch again. He really did not like that determined look in the other werewolf's inhuman eyes.

Both Earl and Jimmy flanked him, wearing variations of camouflage outfits similar to their leader's. "Good morning!" Davey greeted them cheerfully, clapped his hands, and eagerly rubbed them together. "I hope you boys rested up, because you're gonna need to be on top of your game today. It's time we started practicing. I have customers who pay quite a lot for a good show, and I think it's time they get their money's worth."

"So is that what this is really about then?" Korban demanded, that fire inside returning now that he could think straight. "You are holding us hostage to play in some sort of fight club fantasy, so you can profit from it?"

Davey's grin only widened at that, clearly happy with his challenge. "Oh, I do more than profit from it, Korban, and thank you for being so kind as volunteering to go first." He looked to his two human companions and snapped his fingers. "Jimmy go lock the door. Earl, unlock our friend Korban's cage."

Jimmy's head bobbed up and down as he obeyed the command without question, but Earl seemed to hesitate. "You sure about this, Davey?" The usual authoritative tone of his drill sergeant persona seemed to evaporate now that he was being asked to unlock Korban's prison.

Davey's smile seemed to remain cheerful, even when he snapped and grabbed Earl by the collar of his faded green t-shirt and snarled in his face. "Did I stutter, brother?"

"N-no, no Davey!" Earl broke into a sweat and his eyes bulged with fear, and just as quickly Davey chuckled, released him, and Earl fumbled with the keys as he retrieved them from his pocket.

Korban gave the suddenly nervous man a slow smile of his own, like baring his teeth in a snarl. It was somewhat refreshing to smell the fear radiating like a perfume from the cocky tough guy. Earl's hands shook and the keys jangled as he unlocked the cage door. "Oh, come on now Earl. Korban's not going to bite you, he's a respectable werewolf. Aren't you, Korban?"

Korban gave a slow nod, but kept his gaze on Earl along with that unwavering, unnerving grin. He calculated his chances. If it was just Earl and Jimmy he could easily take them out, but Davey's eyes were locked on his every movement, and more than likely he would stop Korban before he could even make it to the door. No, this wasn't the time to escape yet. But the time would present itself if he played along and gained Davey's trust. Maybe he could still talk some sense into him. Or at least make him reveal something that could be useful to aid in his escape. Their escape, he thought quickly. He wouldn't leave the others to this fate if he could help it.

Earl opened the door and strode as quickly as he could out of Korban's reach, over behind where Davey stood. The amusement never left those wolfish eyes as he beckoned him over with a curl of his fingers. "Come on out, Korban."

The way he said his name was almost too cheerful, a mocking tone. What was Davey's real game here? He stepped forward anyway, cautious, still not trusting the look in the werewolf's eyes. They were more wolfish than human, even compared to his own, especially with the look that was in them now.

Predatory. Waiting. Watching.

Korban swallowed anxiously as Davey's hands curled into fists. He stepped out of the cage, and wondered if the others had stopped breathing. All eyes were on the two of them as they circled one another. Earl kept his distance. From the corner of his eye he spotted Jimmy holding a rifle steady on him. He chose his words carefully, and trying to keep things light, he joked, "I'd probably be able to concentrate more on our um, fisticuffs, if I had a pair of pants on."

Davey paused at his request, blinked, and then suddenly tossed his head back and guffawed loudly, the sound filling the room. Jimmy and Earl flinched at the sound; the true laughter from their leader startled them. Perhaps it had been awhile since he had gone with something other than his maniacal laugh. "You continue to surprise me, Korban Diego. All right. Go get him some pants Earl. I have a pair of sweat pants in my gym bag out in the truck. I suppose you'll be a much greater challenge if we aren't doing this Greco-Roman style."

Earl didn't look too happy to be given another order, but he wisely kept any complaints to himself, then turned and headed toward the door where Jimmy stood guard. Korban was tempted to make another run for it, watched as the door opened and closed, and for the first time caught a glimpse of the outer hall. From the scent that slipped in he recognized they were still somewhere in the mountains. Something about this revelation gave him a tiny sliver of comfort. At least he wasn't too far away from where Sophie was, or so he hoped.

Korban gazed to Davey, who he'd managed to stall. Maybe he could get some answers from the man – or wolf – himself. "Why are you doing this? Holding us hostage, making us fight like dogs?"

Davey's cold smile returned. "Because it's fun. You telling me you aren't having fun here, Korban? Well, I suppose that's kind of my fault. Not introducing myself right away, and the usual wolves we bring in, well…" He trailed off a moment, let his gaze wander over to the other cages and the men contained within. "They need to be broken in a little."

"So you starve them and dehydrate them, until they give in and fight you?" he asked, disgusted by how callous Davey seemed about torturing others.

"Oh, it's not just about the fight," Davey circled him, his tone matter-of-fact, "It's about letting them know who's in charge here. It's a matter of teaching respect. Tell me, Korban, are you treated with respect where you come from?"

Korban opened his mouth to speak, but then thought about it. He was tethered to another human being who was legally responsible for everything he did. RJ was probably being punished as they spoke for his indiscretions, regardless of his motive to rescue Sophie. Society at large treated him even more like an outcast because he couldn't hide what he had become. The endless string of job interviews, of trying to piece his life back together with the odds stacked against him.

He nodded, but Davey smirked again and called his bluff. "You had to really think about that, didn't you? Well, in here, it's a brave new world. You earn your respect through battle. It's the way God intended for us to be! None of this corporate, bureaucratic bullshit that they raised us to believe in. Do a good job and follow the laws that weak men in overpriced suits made, to keep their own manicured mitts from getting dirty! There's nothing more satisfying than settling an issue with ah, how did you put it? Fisticuffs?" He chuckled again at the word, and shook his head as he circled around him once more. "Respect is earned in the ring. Not through some rich man's game. It's won when you crack your knuckles into someone's jaw, spill their blood and teeth out. And as a wolf, well… that certainly opens up a lot of opportunities to spill blood and earn a hell of a lot of respect."

Dread crept up on Korban, and he swallowed nervously at Davey's words. Words that he spoke with such conviction. "So you don't have a sponsor? How did you get out of quarantine?"

"I don't need some handler to call the shots for me." Davey's grin widened, his yellow eyes bright with madness.

Before he could say more, the door opened again and Earl returned with a pair of dark gray sweat pants, which he tossed to Korban at some distance. Korban caught the pants and pulled them on quickly, feeling better now that his more personal bits were covered up and less exposed. "Thanks."

"All right then." Davey cracked his knuckles and his bright yellow eyes light up with excitement. "Let's begin day one of our training. Fight night is coming up and I want to make sure we're all ready... so today we're going to take time to stretch our legs... and have a nice run in the woods. A hunt."

Korban blinked and stared at him. He'd expected several other things, but this... this felt like a trap.

Davey walked over to Blaze's cage and Earl flanked him, retrieving the keys from his pocket again. They glinted silver as he unlocked Blaze's cage, and it dawned on Korban then that they must have been silver coated to keep someone from stealing the keys and making an escape. It seemed like they had thought of everything, so the fact that he wanted them to run in the forest free now made him even more suspicious. "My Blaze, my champion... you of all my wolves deserves a chance to stretch his legs," Davey purred as Earl opened the door. "Come out."

Blaze said nothing, just frowned and stepped forward, out of the cage. His hands were curled into fists that shook at his sides as he stood there.

As Davey walked over to Spike's cage with Earl, Korban felt his stomach sink. What was the catch here? He didn't trust this at all. Of course, the idea of being able to run free was a tempting one. He could run, and fast. He would be able to put a lot of distance between himself and Davey. He could escape, go find help, and get the others out of this psychopath's *Fight Club* fantasy. "Spike, you need the exercise. We'll get you in shape soon enough! Or you'll end up as a whole lot of fatty meat on the Pit floor."

Spike didn't say anything, just hung his head in shame as he emerged from his cage, his eyes on his round belly. His hands shook even more than Blaze's did.

Davey reached Hati's cage and paused. "Our new wolf almost got away from us last time we raced. I admire your speed, but we can't risk that again," he smirked to Earl. "Then again, it was fun to chase you down and put you back in your place. Let's keep things interesting. Go ahead, open up his cage. Let's see if our pup here has learned since his last lesson in humility."

Hati averted his gaze and looked down, clearly unhappy by the reminder but not saying anything. Not one of the three men who were imprisoned here seemed to want to upset Davey. Hell, his human friends were careful not to do it either. He squared his jaw and his hands shook worse than Blaze's, but he stepped out like the other two did and stood there with his eyes focused on the floor.

Davey laughed again, rubbed his hands eagerly as he headed over to the main entrance. He walked backwards so he could keep his eyes on all of them, and Korban felt that creepy sensation course through him again as those wolf-like eyes focused on him. "All right, gentlemen... wolves... it's time to get this hunting party started!" He opened the door, stepped aside and rolled his shoulder, flexed a muscle, and stretched in a fluid, cat-like motion. "On your mark... get set... GO!"

12: CHASE

Korban didn't hesitate. It was like the word unsnapped an invisible collar from his throat, and he ran. The three other werewolves with him bolted, and together they ran for the door. Trap or no trap, he couldn't throw away this shot to escape.

Beyond the door was a curved, empty hall. It wound around the building and at first seemed to circle back around to where they had started like some twisted maze; only the scent of wild forest, fragrant fresh air greeted them when they raced around. Up ahead of them a set of double doors were opened wide and bright sunlight shone in like a beacon of hope.

Free at last Korban nearly gave a howl of joy as he emerged from the building that had become his prison. Adrenaline rushed through him as he ran with renewed exhilaration. His eyes adjusted quickly to the glaring light. The building he emerged from was a large red barn in the middle of an expansive clearing. Two large, rust-mottled pickup trucks were parked nearby, alongside a dilapidated house and a shed surrounded by a cluster of ATVs in various states of repair. No powerlines attached to the buildings, and no roads except a few overgrown dirt paths were to be seen. They were completely off the grid. Of course an escape from here wouldn't be easy. He raced towards the tree line, past the vehicles, the lush green forest calling his name.

His muscles screamed at him from being caged and sedentary but he sprinted forward despite the pain, desperate to put as much distance as he could between that prison and himself. The trees and brush became green blurs as he moved, his heart beating like constant thunder in his head. This area of the forest smelled much like the rest he'd experienced before, and judging by the sights and scents he was still somewhere in the Adirondack Mountains.

A large stream suddenly cut out in front of him and caused him to stumble to a halt, scattering rocks along the creek bed as he stopped to keep himself from falling in. The water didn't seem too deep so he said, "I think we can wade across it guys."

He turned to face his fellow escapees, but no one was there. He panted, strained his ears to listen, but he could only hear the babbling brook and the quiet song of the forest. He didn't hear any branches snapping or footsteps rushing behind him and his heart sank. "Guys?"

There was still no response, and he swallowed then tried to catch his breath. His entire body shook, adrenaline coursing through his veins. His heart was pounding like a frantic drum, so loud he was sure it would give his position away as he crouched among the tall reeds along the riverbank.

He waited, but didn't hear or otherwise sense any sign of the others' approach. Part of him wanted to continue on, to turn and keep running further away. He had to find Sophie, he had to get home. RJ's freedom depended on his return, he was sure of it. He had to make things right.

He started to step down into the creek when a pang of guilt hit him hard. Could he really continue on and leave the others behind with those psychopaths? Would he be able to live with himself knowing he'd abandoned them to some twisted fate?

That same part that urged him to continue running growled at him, *Keep going, get help, come back.*

A sharp whistle pierced through the quiet of the forest, followed by a familiar voice. "Korban! Look out!"

Hati's warning came too late. As he turned in the direction of his fellow prisoner's voice, from the opposite side Spike lunged at him, tackled him down hard and caused them both to land with a splash into the muddy bank of the creek bed. The wind was knocked from Korban's lungs as the heavier werewolf pinned him down beneath the shallows and caused him to choke and sputter for air. "What... the... hell, Spike?" He coughed, suddenly drenched in the muddy water.

When he glared at Spike the heavy set werewolf trembled, looking more fearful than ever. "I-I'm sorry, Korban, he made me do it. I can't disobey him. I'm so sorry."

Before Korban could argue further, suddenly Spike got up, grabbed him up by the upper arm, and yanked him back toward the shore. Korban jerked back his arm but suddenly found Blaze there too, grabbing his other arm as he silently frowned. Korban struggled to free himself from the pair but they were dragging him back, almost robotically, neither saying much more. Hati stepped behind the three of them, and when Korban turned to catch a glimpse at him he saw his jaw squared, teeth grinding as they headed back through the forest. They headed back up the path towards where they'd been captured before. "What... why are we going back? What the hell, Spike? Let me go, let's get out of here, all of us! Right now! What are you waiting for?" Korban barked out, and for a moment it seemed Spike did hesitate, but Blaze shoved him forward.

"Do us all a favor and put a sock in it," Blaze cautioned, then fell silent again as they broke through the brush and growth of the forest and returned to the clearing where Davey stood, arms folded over his chest and a sly smirk spread across his face, flanked by his two human goons.

"My, my, my... look what my wolves have returned with! Did you really think I'd let you go so easily, Korban?" Davey clucked his tongue and shook his head, that smile never wavering. "Not a chance would I give up my most prized wolf to date... let's get you all back inside, get some dinner and drinks in you for a hunt well played... and then I think we'll pick up our training tomorrow." He licked his teeth, in the same way a predator cleaned their fangs after a kill. "I already can't wait to see how you'll handle our next game."

~*~

The sun was beginning to set again, the sky turning from pale blue to orange, tinges of violet and lavender creeping up toward the highest point in the sky. With the changing of the sky signaling another day of fruitless searching coming to an end, Sophie's heart sank in time with the sun behind the distant hills. When they returned to the camp she felt like howling out her frustration, but with darkness closing in, Val's words of caution to return to camp seemed to echo in her mind. She didn't want to sleep or eat. She wanted to be out there searching for Korban, until he was found. Until she knew he was safe and also had some safe place to sleep or rest, and something to eat or drink, she wanted to keep going.

She began to pace as the rest of Odin's pack gathered around the camp fire for the night to go over their lack of findings that day. "Sophie, you should sit. Try to relax. It's not going to help him or you for that matter if you wear yourself out. You need your strength for tomorrow." Val's tone sent an even more frustrating feeling through her— that reasonable tone of voice that parents used with defiant children, when their child knew they were right but hated to admit it.

Sophie found herself sitting and staring into the fire, listening to snippets of the all too familiar conversation. They were running out of ideas. She could only hope that inspiration would come. Instead, she thought back to a time where she was sitting at a smaller camp fire, curled up on a cold, clear night snug in Korban's warm lap.

Even now she could feel his arms around her, could feel his warm breath on her ear as he chuckled at something she'd joked about. The memory made her smile, just like she had smiled then.

The smell of burning wood and the warm, welcome scent of him flooded her senses. Familiar forest, fragrant pine, and musk of wolf fur. She closed her eyes and almost felt his strong arms around her once more. She must have started to drift off to sleep, because the next thing she knew, Val peered over to her, a frown etched on her face. "Sophie, why don't you go in the trailer and get yourself a hot shower? Maybe it will help you relax and recharge."

Some time alone to clear her head sounded good, so she nodded and after Val got her a fresh set of clothes to put on and a clean towel, she cranked on the tiny shower, stripped, and then stepped inside. The hot stream of water felt divine, though she would trade it in a heartbeat to be back in the chilly lake with only Korban there to warm her up. She poured shampoo into her palm and mixed in a few drops of conditioner, the coconut scent familiar. Val's signature scent. She could feel herself relax, though as the steam fogged up the glass on the tiny window and mirror above the sink, her mind began to wander again.

Where was Korban now? Was he able to enjoy a hot shower? Was he safe, and just as worried about her as she was for him? They would laugh together about it when they were reunited.

When the rivulets of water at her feet no longer carried bubbles and suds, she turned off the hot water and then dried off before she put on the fresh set of clothes. She toweled off her hair, and it was still damp as she headed out of the trailer and said good-night to the others before she hid away in her tent once again. She lay down and for a long moment stared at the bag of Korban's clothes which sat there next to her pillow. She pulled out his borrowed t-shirt, pulling it closer to her and breathed in his faded scent as she closed her eyes.

She found herself out in the forest again, in the clearing with the trailer where they had camped together before the full moon. The familiar silver Streamline sat there, a constant sentinel in that clearing. It was there long before they arrived, and would be there a long while after they left these mountains. "Sophie," Korban's voice came from behind her, and her heart soared as she spun around.

Instead of her boyfriend being there, a familiar and massive gray wolf stood at the edge of the clearing, his tail held tall and ears perked up. Her heart skipped a beat as she recognized his wolf form, and she breathed a small sigh of relief. "Korban, it's you."

He gave a small wag of his tail in confirmation, then his voice came again as he turned towards the forest. "I love you."

"I love—" Sophie began, but he bolted away, the leaves and brush swallowed him whole as he raced off. "Korban! Wait!" She cried out as she rushed off after him.

Beyond the clearing, the forest became a mirror maze of trees and green foliage. Everything seemed to look the same as she raced after him. Her throat tightened as she lost sight of his tail, and she suddenly found herself alone and lost once again.

"Korban!" She called to him, pleaded. "Korban, where are you?"

There came a rustle ahead of her and she felt a brief moment of relief as golden eyes peered from behind the brush at her. "Korban, you scared me…" She stopped again as instead of a gray wolf another wolf stepped out, with light golden fur. She tensed, but there was something familiar about this wolf too. She remembered a much more vicious dream where she had seen her before, this wolf was her.

The golden wolf trotted over to her, whimpered, tail curled between her legs in submission as she approached. Sophie froze, not sure if her own wolf would attack her. The she-wolf kept her head low as she went over, and then nudged Sophie's hand. She turned, as if to gesture for Sophie to follow her. Sophie nodded, silent, and followed as the golden wolf slowly lead the way through the brush, and returned her to a familiar path. Sophie recognized it as one of the paths that lead from Odin and Valkyrie's camp.

Sophie watched carefully as the golden wolf lead her through the forest. This was all familiar to her she realized as she noted the landmarks she recognized from the days of searching for their missing pack mates. Her wolf form turned and made sure she was still behind her as she guided her from the familiar path to a new one, still moving slowly through the lush greens. This was a new trail but there was something also familiar to it. She saw a snapped set of twigs, and though her scent had faded here, she could smell it faintly, a trace of mint and vanilla. She had been here, maybe running from the full moon night. Her heart soared again.

The golden wolf sensed her recognition and her tail unfurled from beneath her, growing in confidence as she led Sophie deeper down the hidden path, winding around past several snapped twigs until they reached another overgrown clearing. Sophie had sped up her steps, but stopped when they reached this clearing when she heard his voice again, closer this time, louder and clearer. "Sophie," Korban's voice came like an echo in her mind, and her eyes set in on the gaping maw of another wolf pit that sprawled before her.

"Korban!" She called back to him, and rushed toward the edge of the wolf pit.

"I love you," his voice came back, as clear in her memory as the first time he'd said it. She slowed so she wouldn't fall in the pit, and peered down inside the deep hole.

"I love you too, Korban!" She called down to him, into the inky darkness of the shadowy pit. "I love you so much!"

Tears filled her eyes, she had finally said it, and she finally admitted it here and now, out loud. Only her joy of finding him and the pit quickly soured as her vision adjusted to the shadows below her. She sank to her knees as her heart broke, and her own wail melted into an anguished howl, or maybe it was the golden wolf mourning alongside her. At the bottom of the pit below laid pale wolf bones.

"No!" Sophie woke with a start, Korban's shirt clutched up against her chest as she sat up, her mouth dry and her eyes wet with tears. "Korban!" She yanked away the blankets and rushed from the tent. She had to find that path. She had to get to him, and now. Before it was too late.

She felt a warning tug as she started from the camp, but the darkness of the middle of the night filled her with less dread than the soft daylight of her nightmare. She had to get down that path while it was fresh in her mind. A voice called to her from the camp but she ignored them. The urgency to find Korban was all she focused on as she headed up the path, then deviated from it where the wolf had guided her in the dream. It was a little more challenging to find the snapped trail of branches in the darkness, but the memory of those bones laying at the bottom of the pit sent panic through her she couldn't shake away.

Sure enough, she found more of the broken branches, the path she must have cleared for herself as she raced away from the pit as a wolf. Patches of memory, from her dream and that night, seemed to fill in the gaps on the path. She soon found herself in that overgrown clearing, and to her horror and awe, there it was, the other wolf pit. The one where Korban had been trapped.

A soft cry escaped her lips and she lurched forward to go see if he was at the bottom of the pit, but a strong hand grabbed her shoulder and held her back. She whirled around and growled in surprise as she came face to face with Val, who frowned at her. "What are you thinking, going out here in the middle of the night, Sophie? You could have fallen into that trap!"

Sophie didn't like to be scolded like a child. "Let me go," she warned the other werewolf with a low growl in her voice.

Something in her look surprised Val, who did let her go, and Sophie walked over to the edge of the pit as both hope and dread filled her. Her eyes adjusted in the dim moonlight, and as she squinted she could see nothing at first. A small click beside her sounded like a shotgun in the silent clearing, and suddenly a tiny spotlight flooded the empty wolf pit below as Valkyrie shone a flashlight down into it.

Empty. Sophie felt another duel of emotions fill her. Relief that there weren't bones abandoned on the smooth rocks below. Heartache that once again though, as she'd reached a dead end in her search.

She sank to her knees as fresh tears blurred her vision and distorted the light that shone below on the vacant trap. Her entire body trembled and she brought a hand up to brush away her tears, only to find a fresh hit of Korban's scent. She'd been so caught up in finding him she had forgotten that she still gripped his shirt. She buried her face into the shirt and sobbed in relief and renewed grief.

Val sat down beside her and put a comforting warm hand on her back, and began to rub soothing circles. As much as she hated her for it moments before, Val's motherly touch was now more than welcome.

13: CONTROL

Night fell, as far as he could tell, and once again Korban found himself in the dark silence of his prison. Only now he was seething with rage, his temper having simmered as the other three wolves remained quiet through their dinner, which he barely touched. He couldn't think of eating when all he kept thinking about was their betrayal. Once Earl and Jimmy left and the lights clicked off, he waited, trying to gather his thoughts. But it kept returning to the moment the three of them had surrounded him and dragged him back to Davey. Captured again, and not a single one of them defied his command.

"I don't get it," he finally growled out loud. "All three of you are working with him? Even though he keeps you prisoner here, and treats you worse than animals?"

Silence again, though he could hear one of them shuffle in the darkness. It only made him angrier, like he was talking to the wall. He raised his voice. "What? Don't want to admit to it? You really are a bunch of spineless cowards! Don't want to say anything because those two morons might come back? What can they really do? Poke us with sticks, shoot us with silver? What the hell, what does it matter anymore? Clearly you don't want to live; you only want to follow Davey, the psychopath werewolf!" Korban began to pace in his cell, fists clenched along with his jaw as he growled out. "I can't believe you guys! Don't you have any will to live, any reason to fight? Why do you blindly follow him?"

His voice seemed to echo in the air as he shouted into the void. He opened his mouth to vent out some more, when Blaze's voice came low and quiet. "We don't have a choice."

His answer surprised Korban and he tilted his head in the darkness. "What?" He blurted.

"We. Don't. Have. A. Choice." Blaze growled again, a little louder this time. "Whatever Davey says, we do. Not because we want to, but because we have to."

This only confused Korban more and he frowned. "I don't understand. You're telling me that he's able to order you around, and you can't fight it?"

"That's what I am saying, mate," Blaze growled again, and this time Korban can hear it in his tone. Blaze wasn't growling because he was angry at him, but because his jaw was trying to clench tight. He was fighting, only Korban didn't see it before, couldn't see it. Blaze was disobeying, just as much as Hati had the day he slid over his plate of food. They were trying to defy Davey's commands, but they physically could only do so much. The horror of it struck him and he stopped his pacing. "So that's why. You guys are fighting him, but can only do so much. How is he controlling you?"

"Wish we knew how," Hati's voice came this time, and Korban could hear the strain in his voice. How had he missed it before?

Korban glanced at the untouched food he'd left on his plate. "Maybe he is drugging us?"

"No," Hati said through clenched teeth. "Davey wants us pure for the fight. No drugs."

"Then… how?" Korban repeated, and this time he wasn't surprised by the silence that followed his question.

How was Davey able to control the other wolves? So far he hadn't felt even remotely compelled by the other yellow-eyed werewolf's words. Though some of Davey's words nagged him once more.

Someone just like me.

Was it because their eyes were the same? What exactly did that mean then? Korban knew he stood out from the other werewolves before, but this was a whole new level. If he was immune to Davey's control, did that mean he was more like Davey than he knew? Was he able to control others with his gaze too, or whatever power Davey held over Spike, Blaze, and Hati? The thought of being able to have such power over others sent a chill through him. He didn't want to force anyone to do something they didn't want to do. What if he had done something like that before and wasn't aware of it? What if he'd used such power on Sophie and didn't know it?

His heart sank at the thought, until another voice inside him growled at him for entertaining such an idea. He wouldn't force anyone to do anything they didn't want to, not like Davey. Davey was using this ability, or power, to manipulate these three werewolves to do his dirty work. Korban wasn't sure how he was doing it, but he would watch closely tomorrow when they trained. He would not be the same as this yellow-eyed demon. He would find out how he was controlling the others, and then he would figure out a way to stop him from doing it. Something deep inside told him that if he was the only one who could stand up to Davey, he was the only one who could stop him once and for all.

~*~

Sophie didn't sleep that night, too many thoughts raced in her head. Part of her was terrified of what fresh nightmare her imagination would summon the moment she drifted to sleep, so instead she sat out by the fire, Korban's shirt still clutched in her hands. Valkyrie sat with her for a while once they returned to camp, comforted her as she broke down. But there were only so many tears she could cry before her heartache turned into a hollow emptiness. She greeted the numbness like an old friend. When the pain had slowly ebbed away, what remained was nothing. And she could think better when there was nothing there to cause her pain.

She knew in her heart that the pit she'd found tonight was the one that Korban had been trapped in the night of the full moon. He'd been so close, and yet so far. Someone had set up those traps, for what purpose she wasn't sure of, but it couldn't be good. If only she could get her hands on whoever it was who had set the wolf pits up to begin with, she could...

That was it. She blinked, her own thoughts interrupted by a fresh idea. She could barely contain herself again and stood up, began to pace by the fire. Val gave her a questioning look and Sophie shared her idea. "Someone set up those wolf pits. If they captured Hati in one, and Korban in another, they may have more out there. Or there may be only a couple of traps. But regardless, they will have to return to set them up again, and they'll have to do it soon, so their scent will fade before the trap is used again. We need to double our surveillance. Let them come to us. Then we can follow them, and see where they lead us."

Val nodded and brightened up at her words. "That's my girl, Sophie. Okay, then this morning we'll start watching both pits. We'll take cover and stakeout in pairs. We'll let these bastards come to us. They better have not hurt either one of our missing men, or they're gonna be sorry."

Over breakfast that morning Val revealed their plan with Sophie, and Odin and the others seemed to approve. They broke off into pairs after deciding a patrol schedule and soon went off to their posts for the day. The little bit of scrambled egg and strip of beef jerky she'd managed to get down in her stomach sat like rocks as Sophie crouched hidden in the brush near the trap she'd uncovered last night. Geri joined her today and she was thankful the quiet, older brother was partnered with her today. She needed to keep her mind clear, her senses on high alert. If they came to reset the trap as she predicted, she would be ready.

She listened to the quiet song of the forest and waited.

Korban tried to sleep despite his growling stomach. As tempted as he was to eat what remained of his dinner, he left it untouched, not entirely convinced yet that Davey wasn't drugging their food to control them. He had his theories, but until he confirmed the truth he would be extra cautious.

To keep his mind off his hollow belly he focused instead on the sweet memories of his time with Sophie. How many days had passed since he woke in this cell? Time moved so differently when you were trapped in nearly constant darkness, and he wasn't sure, but it had been too long since he had held her in his arms. He never knew what it meant to long for someone until now. He missed the way her soft curves fit against him, the way her skin smelled faintly of mint, the sweet taste of her lips on his. He would give everything, anything, just to have more time with her, even cramped up in that old silver Streamline. Their temporary home felt like a palace compared to this place.

Though his thoughts lingered as long as he would let them on his Mate, his mind always returned with a fresh set of worries. Was Sophie safe now out there, searching for him? Did she find help by now? Maybe the cavalry was on its way.

But what if she was still alone, looking for him, and she fell victim to one of Davey's traps?

He had to figure out how to stop Davey. If by some chance Davey was to get his claws on her… the mere thought evoked a vicious growl from Korban. He would never, ever let that monster touch Sophie. Not as long as his heart was still beating.

His busy mind finally drifted off to a fitful sleep when the familiar metallic click of the lock on the door cracked loudly in the dark echo chamber of their prison. Instead of immediately sitting up to face his enemy, Korban fought the urge to look as the lights clicked on and the steady hum of the fluorescent bulbs filled the air. He feigned sleep as Davey walked over to their cages; his eyes opened a slight crack, silent as he watched him carefully through his thick eyelashes. Earl and Jimmy followed him in but remained silent as they stood guard by the door. "Good morning, my wolves!" Davey greeted them cheerfully, and at the sound of his voice Korban could see Blaze and Spike sit up in attention. "I hope you slept well," he paused and smirked over at Korban, "though it looks like maybe our new friend slept a little too well."

His gaze didn't linger long on him; instead it went to Blaze as he approached the British werewolf's enclosure. "Good morning, Blaze. Tell me, how's my favorite fighter doing today?"

Korban let his eyes open a little more to observe, and he watched through carefully lidded eyes as Blaze's hands shook and his jaw squared, but he lifted his head to meet Davey's gaze. "Dandy," Blaze growled the word, unable to remain silent but fighting back from giving Davey the luxury of a true response.

Davey chuckled in amusement and then walked over to Spike's cage. "Spikey, Spikey, Spike… how about you?"

The rotund werewolf whimpered, and without being further prompted, he blurted out, "I'm good, Davey, s-sir."

Davey stood there, still facing away from Korban so he couldn't see his expression, but he could hear the amusement in his voice as he jingled the key in his pocket. Perhaps his set of keys weren't silver coated after all. "I hope you're ready for today, big fella."

Spike lowered his gaze down to the ground and his lower lip trembled. Whatever hold on him Davey had, it still sent fear through the large man. Korban felt a surge of protectiveness for the other wolf as he cowered, but bit his lip to keep from opening his mouth.

Davey walked over to Hati's cage, out of Korban's view, so he tried to casually stretch to keep his gaze on the other wolf. Once again Davey paused in front of the pen. He was quiet for a long moment, but then he chuckled softly. "Well, you aren't really the new guy any more, but you certainly did impress me yesterday. I bet today you'll continue to show me what you can do. Won't you?" He turned then and his yellow eyes fixed on him at last. "Time to wake up my newest friend so we can get started."

There was no need to play pretend any more. Korban stretched again and blinked open his eyes. He was careful to avoid Davey's gaze for a moment, letting his eyes focus instead on that confident smirk that spread across his face. "Now that you're all awake, we can start the second day of our training." Davey rubbed his hands together eagerly. "I want to see exactly how strong you really are Korban... so it's going to be you and me in the ring. I think it's time you show me what you got."

"You don't have to do this, Davey," Korban tried as the werewolf pulled out the key to his cage.

"Such a pacifist." Davey made a disgusted face, and as the lock clicked, he pulled the door open. "There's nothing to discuss. Come out and let's get to it. I need to see how much training you're going to need before fight night."

"I don't want to fight you, Davey," Korban said, and stood, taking a step back, not that he could really go far to avoid him. His stomach twisted into a fresh knot of anxiety. He wasn't much of a fighter, and preferred to avoid conflict when possible. Sure, he had thrown a few punches in defense of his friends, such as the one he'd landed on the jerk bodyguard Matt who had grabbed onto Sophie during their first encounter at Howl at the Moon. It didn't mean he was Rocky Balboa. "Davey, please. We can talk this out."

Davey's amused light in his eyes flashed to one of anger. It was like hitting a light switch, and he moved faster than any normal man could or should. If Korban wasn't a werewolf, he was certain the breeze he dodged – where Davey's fist striking out past him – would have knocked him hard across the floor. "I don't have to do anything. I want to, Korban. I want to fight you. And you'll fight me, or you'll be beaten to a pulp." Davey growled, then stepped back from the doorway and gestured with his hand. "Come out Korban. Neither one of us needs silver burns to add injury to insult."

Davey stepped back again, his yellow eyes narrowed and focused intently on Korban. He felt his skin begin to crawl under that gaze, and knew that Davey would fight him, regardless of whether he was in the silver-coated cage or not. Better to avoid the extra damage if he could, though he was cautious as he stepped out into the open space. He felt the eyes of the other werewolves from the cages that circled him. "Please Davey," he said and held up his hands. "I'm not a fighter."

"All men are fighters, deep down." Davey licked his lips, eagerness reflected over his anger. "It's what we crave as human beings. It's human nature. Not the wolf, though the wolf side can be just as bloodthirsty as we are, at times. Just not as brutal as we are as men."

Davey suddenly stepped forward and swung his fist. Korban narrowly dodged the strike, but then Davey launched another violent punch, followed rapidly by another, and another. Korban quickly stepped backward, his hands raised up defensively to stop his blows, and though he avoided them so far, he knew his luck would run out. His heart and mind raced for a solution, but unfortunately Davey's words were right. In the end, words wouldn't reach this man. Not the way violence would. Still, he would try his best to show him another way.

Davey's fist soared towards his jaw in an uppercut, but Korban twisted out of the way, his eyes narrowing as he suddenly moved his hand and caught his fist with it. A surge of power coursed through his knuckles and up his arm, and as he gripped Davey's curled hand, his knuckles turned white. Davey moved fast, his free hand launching toward Korban's stomach. Korban's hand wasn't fast enough to block the blow, and his fist connected. The wind was knocked from him and Korban curled forward with a loud gasp. His head jerked upward as he gasped for air, and his eyes locked with Davey's, amusement and triumph reflected in those bright yellow orbs.

This close his eyes were as vibrant as the sun, and once again his skin crawled, as if thousands of ants marched over his flesh. A dizzy sensation jolted through him, maybe from the lack of oxygen. He gasped like a fish on land. There was an odd feeling of weightlessness that only seemed to grow as he gripped Davey's fists and their gaze remained locked. Davey's eyes seemed to glow brighter, as a victorious laugh escaped him and filled the air, only it was cut short, and a look of confusion mirroring his own filled those wolf-like eyes.

The strange sensation of detachment only intensified, and the next thing Korban knew he found himself floating, lost in a spiral of bright yellow light. He closed his eyes and embraced the darkness he knew would come.

The strange out-of-body-like experience only seemed to continue even when a quiet darkness took hold. Was he dead? Had Davey killed him somehow? Korban felt disoriented, the darkness rippled around him like waves. His stomach hurt, but maybe it was still sore from being punched. The odd feeling of gravity leaving him didn't help much with the nausea.

Images began to flash before his eyes as he stood there, caught in a moment of time that seemed to span forever. It reminded him at first of the same way his wolf saw the full moon night. Only these images, first blurry and hazy like from an old movie projector, soon came into focus and played before him like a clip show, except he felt like a shadow on the wall, a silent witness to the scenes that played before him as each one grew into focus beyond high definition.

First came a faded moment that felt vintage as it came into focus on two lanky little boys he'd never seen before. There was something familiar about the mop of brown hair on the smaller boy, and the way he smiled as he stared down at a deer that was limping at the bottom of a pit trap. "Stay back from there, you don't wanna fall down into that," the older boy cautioned as he walked over and slid the long rifle off his shoulder. "If you go breaking a leg I'll get in trouble and I don't want Dad mad at me again because of you."

"What is it?" the younger boy asked as he took a step back.

The older boy rolled his eyes. "It's a wolf pit."

"A wolf pit? But a deer is in it."

Exasperated, the older boy grunted as he loaded the gun. "Duh, it's a deer. It's just what it's called. It's used to help us hunt things."

The boy thought about that and tilted his head. "Has Dad ever caught a real wolf in it?"

"There aren't wolves around here. Not anymore." The older boy aimed the rifle and shot the deer. "Come on; help me get it out of there so we can clean it." The scene faded as the taller boy ushered him away from the pit and toward where they parked their ATVs.

The darkness swallowed him again, and he floated through another scene. This time the pair of boys were older, taller and standing together silently, both wearing black as a coffin was lowered into the ground in front of them. They didn't have suits but instead wore faded black jeans. The smaller boy wore a black t-shirt inside out, and stared blankly with almost a bored look as the coffin sank into the ground. The older boy beside him fought back tears and squeezed his hand. The image was still grainy, like this was from a while ago, but this time the images came with the faint smell of rain and freshly dug dirt.

As the coffin was lowered, the image split and he could smell cheap liquor and cigarette smoke in the air. While the funeral continued on in the one faded panel, a new scene came to light in the next. A thin woman with blue eyes and light brown hair prematurely graying sat on the edge of the younger boy's bed with a book in her hands. She was reading a story to him and the pale, skinny boy was listening raptly. There was a smell beneath the alcohol and tobacco that Korban was familiar with and it turned his stomach. Sickness. The boy, or the woman, or both, were extremely ill. "Some tribes believed that by consuming the flesh of their enemies, they would gain their strength," she read to him as she puffed on a thin cigarette.

She paused and took a long drag, and the boy asked softy, "Is that true, Mom?"

"What?" she coughed and sputtered.

"If you eat someone you beat in battle, do you get stronger?" the thin boy asked.

"I dunno, Davey," the woman shrugged as she managed to get her smoker's cough under control. "I ain't never ate any of my enemies so I wouldn't know. But stranger things have happened I suppose. History is kinda weird like that."

The boy coughed and looked at the book. "Read it again?"

I will never be weaker than my enemies. Korban tensed as he heard the thought out loud, and an intense look filled Davey's blue eyes as he watched them bury his mother. Korban could feel Davey's resolve strengthen with every word, and sensed every emotion along with the boy. *I will never be weak again.*

The smells and light faded and he was lost to the shadows again. Years passed by in flickering moments, moving faster and faster. He was dizzy with all of the pictures that grew in intensity as they rushed past. Davey was growing up. The older boy, Earl, grew up too. He taught his brother to hunt and use the wolf pits to trap animals, and more importantly, how to get the animals out. The images slowed down when one day Davey discovered not a deer or animal in one of his traps, but a hunter. The man was drunk and lost, and had broken his arm in the fall. He was in a foul mood and swore at Davey when he approached. "You sonuvabitch! Get me outta here!" The man slurred, and when Davey got the rope and pulled him up the man punched him across the jaw.

Davey stumbled, but regained his balance quickly, and a slow smile spread across his face as he licked his own blood from the corner of his mouth. He lunged for the man and began to fight him. He put up an admirable struggle, but in the end the drunken hunter ended up swinging hard for Davey and lost his balance. He fell back down into the wolf pit with a sickening crunch.

Davey tilted his head curiously, went over to the edge of the pit, and looked down. The man laid dead, his head bent at a wrong angle. "I defeat my enemy... and devour the soul of a warrior," he said very softly as his smile widened.

The darkness twisted around him again, like thick plumes of smoke. More images flashed by, more unlucky souls who found themselves lost in the Adirondacks and into one of Davey's wolf pits. He learned how to hide them better, and learned how to bring them back. Lost hikers and hunters who were unfortunate enough to fall into one of his pits ended up as pawns in his game.

Whatever was happening now, it was happening faster. The images blurred again, and the shadows surrounded and swallowed Korban.

Just as suddenly Korban found himself no longer in darkness, but in the crisp, clean mountain air of the forest once more. The sky was clear and the sun streamed down around him. He felt the warmth of the rays of light as they poured down from the green canopy of leaves above him. He smelled the fragrant pine and leaves, the musk of the animals that scurried through the trees and brush. Yet when he held up his hand he could see the ground through his skin, muscle, and bone. That sinking feeling filled him again. Did Davey finish him off, and this was what it was like to die? It would explain the strange out of body experience he seemed to be having, and the bright light. But weren't you supposed to see your own life flash before your eyes, not someone else's? He couldn't be dead! There was still so much he had to do in his life! He had to help the others escape Davey, and he had to see Sophie again!

Before he could say anything to protest this injustice, something caught his attention. A low, anguished moan came from nearby. It sounded like a creature was caught somewhere and in pain. Korban turned and headed toward the sound. The trees and brush gave way to a familiar clearing, and an even more familiar large, rectangular hole carved into the ground. It was the wolf pit he'd fallen victim to, where this nightmare had all started. In the bright morning light the clearing seemed peaceful, except for that gaping maw of the trap and the pained cries coming from within it.

Was this his fate, to relive this hell for eternity? His throat tightened as he cautiously stepped over to the edge of the pit, and peered down inside. Down in the dark depths a naked stranger with a mop of shaggy, red hair and blue eyes lay twisted in a broken net, moaning as he tried to stand up. In the same warm sunlight Korban could see now that the man's leg was broken and twisted beneath him, obscenely healed in all the wrong ways from the fall in this wolf trap. He watched on in horror as the man – a wounded werewolf – tried to break his own leg to set it right again.

"Well, well, well… what have we here?" Davey's voice came from behind him, and Korban froze in his tracks.

Even in death it seemed he hadn't escaped this monster.

14: WITNESS

Korban gasped and stepped back from the pit as Davey leered at him, but then moved past him as if he were an unseen ghost and peered down into the wolf pit. "Nasty business, these old wolf pits. Are you all right down there?" Davey called down into the trap with that same amusement reflected in his twisted grin.

"Thank God!" The stranger in the pit sobbed in relief. "Please, please help me. Help me out. Please!"

Davey tilted his head as curiosity filled his eyes. His eyes! Korban realized that they were still a bright blue. Not the unearthly yellow that he was accustomed to now. Korban wondered how this was possible and he came to terms with all that he had seen so far. Somehow he was now a silent witness to another piece of Davey's past, instead of battling him in the present within the prison he'd created. Stunned and in awe, he watched as the scene before him unfolded.

"No problem, my friend. Though you really should be more careful out here. You know there are all sorts of strange beasts this far in the forest. Bears, wolves… some even say cannibals live out here, did you know that?" He chuckled at the joke, licked his lips, and gazed down at the trapped man. "I've seen a lot of strange things in my time living out here… but this definitely tops it all! What a lucky day to be alive."

The stranger nervously laughed, not seeming to grasp the dire situation he was in. Of course, Korban hadn't understood either how devastating it was to be caught in Davey's wolf trap when he woke up in it. "Ha, yeah, it's funny how things… end up this way… so, can you help me out, buddy? I need help to set my leg and then I can be on my way. I won't be any bother at all."

Every word that came out of this man was tinged with pain, but it didn't seem to faze Davey. "Of course you won't be a bother! You're my guest!" Davey laughed again and the cold sound seemed to mock real laughter as he crouched down near the edge of the wolf pit. "What kind of man would I be, if I didn't take care of my guests?" He stood back up and gave the man a cheerful smile. "I'll just grab some rope and help you out of there."

"Bless you, thank God you're here!" The pained man in the wolf pit's voice filled with such relief that Korban felt a pang of pain in his heart.

Korban watched as Davey whistled a happy tune that was vaguely familiar and strode over to his ATV which was parked nearby. He opened up the seat and began to shuffle around inside of it, and retrieved a brown burlap bag. He opened up the sack and pulled out a small axe that glinted in the sunlight. Still whistling to himself, he pulled out a long coil of rope, which had metal hooks attached to each end. He turned around and whistled as he headed back toward the pit, axe and rope in his hands. He snapped the hook in place on one of the metal hoops on the edge of the pit and it fit like a missing puzzle piece.

"No!" Korban shouted, but neither Davey nor the man reacted to his warning. He really was a silent witness here, able to sense and feel everything, including the eagerness that rolled from Davey as he wrapped the rope around his hip, where along his belt Korban noticed a large sheathed knife.

Korban rushed over to the edge of the pit, and in a desperate move to try and rescue the werewolf inside, he grabbed the side of the wall and lowered himself into the hole. When he let go and let himself fall a few feet down into the trap, he still seemed to float, and to his own horror when he rushed over to the fallen werewolf, his hands moved right through him. There was nothing he could do, this scene had happened before, and now he was here to watch it all unfold. Some twisted memory of Davey's, though how this was happening Korban didn't know. He tried to pinch his arm but his translucent fingers went through his skin. He wasn't waking up from this nightmare.

Relief flooded the werewolf's eyes as Davey lowered himself down with his rope. His heart sped up when he spied the axe, which Davey swung and snapped through the ropes that hung like some obscene spider's web. "I owe you so much for this," the stranger said. "What can I do to repay you? You've saved my life."

Korban's heart thundered in his ears and he wished he was back outside of this pit. He wanted to run far away from this obscene moment in time. He didn't want to see Davey get turned into a werewolf. This stranger didn't realize just how many lives he ruined by biting into this sadist.

Davey only smiled, hooking the axe onto his belt as he bent down and offered a hand up to the wounded werewolf. "You're awfully optimistic, friend," Davey's smile darkened, and in a swift motion his silver blade sliced across the surprised werewolf's throat.

Confusion and fresh pain filled the stranger's eyes as blood poured down his neck, and bubbled from his mouth as he mouthed the word, "Why?"

"People don't understand what it's like to live out here. Meat is meat when it stumbles into one of my traps." Davey licked the blood that splattered onto his lips and it made Korban's stomach queasy. "And something tells me your flesh is going to taste extra special."

Korban turned away as the werewolf's blood garbled howl filled the air, thankfully short lived as Davey finished him off. The wet sound of a knife slicing through raw meat brought him to a new level of hell. His nausea returned to full strength when he was unlucky enough to catch a glimpse of Davey as he chewed on a bloody piece of flesh, the excitement and pleasure of it rolling off Davey like strong cologne.

Davey's laughter filled the wolf pit and seemed to echo around him, and that weightless feeling returned as the world spun around him again. Korban blinked, tried not to vomit as he found himself once again in the building that held his prison. The sensation of returning to his body was worse than the punch to the gut he'd just endured. Davey was sitting across from him, a cold smile spread across his face as he laughed again. "Korban, you continue to surprise me!"

Korban rolled onto his hands and knees and lost what little was in his stomach onto the dirt along the floor. He panted, sweat poured down his forehead, and Davey continued to laugh. "What… the hell… was that?" Korban managed to sputter as he coughed and caught his breath.

"I have no idea, but now I get why you're so eager to get out of here! You were holding out on me, Korban— you rascal! You didn't tell me you weren't alone in the forest!" Ice suddenly moved in Korban's veins as he realized that while he was seeing Davey's past, Davey must have seen his too. Eagerness was reflected in those yellow eyes, the same look he had while he devoured that wounded werewolf. "Sophie, is it? I do look forward to meeting her."

"No," Korban moaned in horror, "leave her out of this!"

"Surely you miss your lady love, Korban. Not that I blame you. There's something kind of exotic about banging a billionaire's wife. And from what I saw, your romantic rendezvous since you got out here has been pretty hot! I get it now; I'd want to get back to that fine piece of ass too." Davey taunted him.

"I won't let you touch her," Korban growled.

Davey only laughed again as he got up on his feet. Korban wanted to hit him, but was afraid of what else he'd see, or worse reveal, to him if he did. If he touched him again, would he return to that nightmare of a memory? His eyes went to the door but Jimmy and Earl had their guns trained on him. He was just as trapped as he had been since he got here, only now it was worse. "Get back into your cage, Korban."

There was an unseen power in those words, the feeling of ants crawling over his skin as the suggestion took hold in his mind. He found himself headed back to the cage, too shocked and raw from the vision he'd witnessed, and what was worse, now Davey knew about Sophie. Sophie. He had to fight this, he had to get out and get her safely back home to Syracuse!

The need to protect her surged through him and strengthened him. He turned to face Davey but the silver bars were suddenly slammed in his face. He regained his senses too late. Davey smirked on the other side of the bars, a triumphant look on his face. Korban grabbed for him but ended up burning his hands on the silver bars, which caused him to yelp as he fell back.

"Don't worry Korban, I'll take really, really good care of her when I find her," Davey promised with a leer that made his skin crawl. "Earl and Jimmy… have you checked the traps recently?"

The two human companions exchanged a glance. "No, Davey…

we haven't reset the traps yet. We were gonna do it this weekend."

"I think you better go get on that pronto boys! We have one foxy werewolf running through the forest, and it would be a shame if we miss out on meeting her because we kept things on the old schedule," Davey said and rubbed his chin thoughtfully. "Of course, you'll be a tough act to follow Korban, but I think I can find ways to convince Sophie that I'm worth it too."

Korban lunged again at the bars, but stopped himself before he touched the silver again. The burns were still healing along his skin, but he couldn't contain his rage. "I swear, I will kill you if you hurt her Davey," he seethed.

"You see Korban? I told you," Davey leaned in, not bothered since he was on the other side of those silver bars. "All men at their core want to fight in the end. I just had to find what moves you. And soon enough... you'll have every reason to give me what I want."

He stepped back and glared at Jimmy and Earl, who still stood there. "What part of pronto don't you understand? Get out there and don't come back until you have those wolf pits reset! If you're lucky enough to catch her, bring her here to me. Though I think maybe I'll need to ah, freshen up for a fine lady like her."

Korban growled, his fists clenched at his sides, but he was utterly helpless as long as Davey had the upper hand. What was worse, the cannibal werewolf knew it. He wouldn't give him the satisfaction if he could help it, though he began to pace in his cage as Davey headed for the door, his two human minions already headed out to set their traps again.

As he paced and tried to chase away the memories of what he'd witnessed in Davey's past, one thought gave him renewed hope despite the situation going from bad to worse. If there was one thing he could count on, it was that as clever as Davey thought he was, there was no way he could fathom just how intelligent Sophie was. If anyone could outsmart that psychopath, it was his Mate.

~*~

Waiting and watching was not what she wanted to do, and every muscle and bone in her itched as she remained hidden in the brush. It wasn't only her wolf she fought against now, but every instinct she had wanted her to keep moving, to keep searching. At least if she moved, it felt like she was doing something that would help find Korban. Sitting here and doing nothing felt like she was going nowhere, and as the hours crept by it only felt more and more like wasted time. She began to question her own plan and was about to protest it herself when she heard it, faint at first, but the distinct rumble of gears brought a cacophony of manmade noise that disrupted the forest song that remained constant around them. An engine to a vehicle, distant at first, but the rumble of metal growing louder as it approached, echoed by a second one as they moved closer in their direction.

She exchanged a glance with Geri, who nodded silently, and the two of them took deeper cover. They kept a close watch as two vehicles approached the clearing. Both ATVs had deeply treaded wheels, and rolled into the clearing with two very different men riding on them. Sophie tensed and suppressed a growl. The muscle-bound man who drove into the clearing first turned the key and shut down the engine to his, while the thinner, lanky man hopped off his camouflaged four-wheeler and walked over to the empty wolf pit. He peered down it and sighed, "No, she ain't in this one."

"Damn shame, I ain't never seen a female werewolf before," the larger man spat on the ground, stood up, and stretched. "I guess we'll be seein' one soon though, won't we?"

Sophie frowned and goosebumps broke out on her skin. She had the distinct impression these two men were talking about her. Of course, if they knew who she was… was it because they had Korban?

She clawed her fingers into the trunk of the tree in front of her to keep herself from attacking the two men then and there. If they did have Korban captive, what was the purpose of it? The one man seemed vaguely militaristic in the way he carried himself, but the pair didn't seem to be secret agents. They came across as more a couple of backwoods hillbillies than men in black who worked for the government, as Odin had predicted.

The thin man pulled out a fresh steak from his backpack and tossed the red, bloody meat down into the center of the pit. It landed with an obscene, wet plop. Something about the scent of raw meat was familiar, venison by what her wolf recalled, but there was something else in it that seemed to draw her attention more, until one of the men's words shook her from the distracting temptation. "If we're lucky it'll be sooner rather than later. You know how impatient Davey gets," the thinner man looked around nervously, then gestured to the rolled up materials on the back of his four-wheeler. "Let's get this one set and then go do the other. I don't like bein' out here when the sun goes down."

"What's the matter? Afraid of a little she-wolf?" The larger man joked as he went over and pulled the rolled up bundles into his strong arms. He carried them over to the edge of the pit without breaking a sweat before he added, "She won't be any different than the other beasts Davey collected. She'll just have a much prettier package when it ain't a full moon, and it won't be a total sausage fest anymore."

The skinny man laughed at that, and with his partner's help they unrolled the bundles which revealed to hold a net with thin silvery chains wrapped around a series of very long, thin sticks. They moved to each side of the wolf pit and spread the net like a blanket over the opening, and bent down to attach the heavier rings to the hooks that lined the pit. Next they carefully set each stick across the trap, until the trap was covered with the twigs. The thinner, younger looking man walked back over to the vehicles and took a couple of the large trash bags off the side, tossing one over to the larger man, who easily caught it. They began to sprinkle dead leaves and cut blades of grass over the sticks, carefully coating the edges so the trap blended in with the ground once again.

Their conversation moved on to mundane things, such as the next race and any sporting events coming up. Sophie watched as they worked, so casually filling in this trap which would so easily claim its next victim if left unchecked. They acted as if this was completely normal, that it was just another day at the office. It made her blood boil how they treated this like it was nothing, when it had caused her and Valkyrie's pack so much suffering.

Geri kept glancing from her to the men, his jaw squared and a serious expression set on his face. He wasn't happy about this either, but he seemed to be torn about going after those two men as they set their trap.

When they were finally satisfied the wolf pit was barely visible once more, the two gathered up what remained of their supplies and revved up their four wheelers before they drove off again into the forest. As soon as the two were out of earshot, Geri turned to Sophie again. "We follow, we don't attack. We need to make sure we find out where these guys are camped out. No matter what happens, we need to stick to the plan. Got it?"

"Got it," Sophie repeated and then they started after the couple of four-wheelers.

They kept their distance as they followed the broken branches and loud engine. Even when they lost the tire tracks due to dry ground or rocky terrain, they could easily track the scents of the two men, or the gasoline and exhaust from the vehicles. When the engines cut out again and silence erupted once more in the forest, they slowed their pace and were careful not to alert the two men that they were being followed. They reached the edge of the next clearing and cautiously peered out, finding them setting the net and sticks across the wolf pit there.

Waiting for them to finish as they reset the trap was somehow worse than waiting around for nothing. So close, and yet so far again.

Sophie began to chew on a fingernail, something she hadn't done since she was in middle school. Her mother wasn't there to reprimand her now, but her voice was a faint echo in her memory. Her heart sank as she wondered if she would ever see her mother again, but she didn't let the thought go long. She had to stay focused, had to track these men and see where they were keeping Korban and Hati. The way these men set the traps without a care, who knew how many others they had? Though she questioned how two human men could do this, especially when they didn't seem all that bright. They had mentioned a Davey, was he their leader? She strained to listen in on their conversation on the other side of the clearing, wishing the full moon was closer so she could hear with ease.

"I hate when we get sent out before we even had breakfast," the muscular one complained as he sprinkled leaves over the loosely set sticks that now lined the wolf pit. "It's almost lunch time and I'm so hungry I could eat the bait."

"Better not." The skinny young man grunted as he heaved up another sack of leaves onto his bony shoulder and went over and covered more of the trap. "Davey will get pissed. He puts his own blood on it too, so unless you want to join his uh, games, as a werewolf too—"

"Shit no! The last thing I want is to be one of his pet wolves," the muscled man seemed to pale at the words alone, and shook his head. "He's my brother and he scares me enough as it is. I don't need his new wolfy voodoo hold over me. I'm fine with things how they is, thank you very much." He paused then shrugged. "I'll grab something when we get back. This won't take long to finish up."

Geri's frown only deepened as he exchanged another silent glance with Sophie at this revelation. Sophie's fists shook as she clenched them. There was no doubt, these men knew where Korban was, and most likely Hati too. If they hurt him, she wasn't sure she would be able to control herself.

Geri nodded to her suddenly, and there came a quiet rustle of leaves as Valkyrie and Freki emerged behind them. Val motioned for Sophie to follow her, and she felt her heels dig in to the ground at the suggestion. She wanted to follow these men and keep them in her sight until she set eyes on Korban once more. Still, something in those yellow eyes urged her, and she suppressed another growl as she followed Val deeper into the forest again.

Thankfully, they didn't move too far away, just enough yards away to be away from human earshot. Val turned to her and whispered, "You looked like you were about to lose it out there. I wanted to make sure you were good for this. We need to follow them, but we can't attack them blind. We need a plan. Are you going to be okay with that, or should we go back to camp now?"

Sophie felt as if Val slapped her, for a moment so insulted she wasn't sure how to respond. Still, she considered her words, relaxed her hands. She felt wetness in her hands and saw her fingernails that she hadn't chewed had dug tiny crescents into her palms. She watched them heal and took a shaky breath. "I will be okay," she said softly, and managed to keep her tone level. "I can't believe… if what they said is true… there is a werewolf, this Davey they talk about. He is behind all this. And if he hurts Korban, I swear I will make him pay for it."

"Yes, he will pay, but we have to be extra careful. For Hati and Korban's sakes," Val began, and Sophie nodded.

"I know Val, I get it. I won't do anything reckless. Not after all we have done to find them." Sophie sighed, and tried to reign in her growing frustration.

"I trust you, Sophie," Val reassured her softly. "I just needed to hear it myself. Your words to my ears. I know you won't go back on your word once you've given it." She paused. "I also wanted to check in, make sure you were okay. Especially after hearing what those two morons were going on about out there."

Sophie smiled sadly and nodded again. "They dropped hints at the other trap that they are looking for a female werewolf. I think they really do have Korban, maybe Hati too. They're still..." She trailed off for a moment as relief choked her off. "I don't know what they are doing to them. But we'll follow them, and find out how to get our guys back safely. We're so close now. I won't mess this up, Val." She met the other werewolf's golden gaze. "I promise you. We're getting our boys back. We're bringing them home."

Val smiled and her eyes brightened at that. She clapped a hand on Sophie's shoulder. "That's what I want to hear. Then there's only one thing we need to do, once we find out where their base..."

The ATV engines screeched back to life and interrupted Val, who pat Sophie on the shoulder once more. "Let's follow them; we'll deal with the rest later. Let's go get our boys back."

Sophie nodded, her determination renewed, and they followed the unsuspecting men on their noisy four wheelers as they headed deeper and deeper into the wilderness.

15: CATALYST

They followed the trail of the raucous four wheelers through the forest until they came to a massive clearing that seemed to come out of nowhere. In the heart of the mountains was a large barn next to a rickety, small farm house that didn't seem to be much larger than the Streamline they had camped in. A rusty pair of pick-up trucks were parked amongst a small cluster of ATVs in various states of repair, and a trailer with a pair of new snowmobiles parked on it. A small shed was next to the house and seemed to be in better shape than the home alongside it, with a massive padlock on the outside. The barn that towered over the house also seemed in far better condition. It was here she suddenly caught it, faint but familiar, and it made her heart flood with hope. Korban's distinct scent was here!

It took all her willpower not to charge toward his scent right then and there. She steadied herself, breathed in that scent she'd longed for since she'd lost him on that full moon night. Not just faded on a borrowed shirt, but a sign that he was recently here. Alive!

Beside her, Freki's nostrils flared and his eyes widened in surprise. "Hati! I can smell him. He's been through here recently." He grinned brightly to Sophie as he whispered, "I smell Korban too. They have to be here!"

She put a finger to her lips and they watched as the two men parked their ATVs alongside the collection of other parked vehicles.

When the skinny man suddenly brandished a rifle from the side of his vehicle, they moved back, slowly, careful not to disturb the tall grass around them too much. Sophie's heart thundered in her ears as she watched the two men head toward the barn and vanish beyond the double doors. Silence fell over the large clearing as the doors closed behind them.

"We need to go after them!" Freki growled, but Sophie shook her head.

"Not yet, we don't know how many of them are in there, and if they have silver bullets or not," her own words were short, clipped, and she had to bite back her own growl as she kept her voice low. "We need to have a plan before we go charging in there."

Val agreed with a nod and a frown. "I don't like it any more than the rest of you, but we're not going to jeopardize their lives when we're this close. Korban and Hati are in there, and we're getting them out. We're going home together." She turned her amber gaze to the small group that gathered there. "So let's keep watch over them and make a plan that won't fail."

~*~

Korban continued to pace and tried to think long after Davey and his commandos had left them alone in the dark again. There had to be a way out of there, a way for him to get free and warn Sophie about Davey. He tried not to panic, to remind himself again that Sophie was smart, and strong, and she could handle herself. But Davey was despicable, cruel, and insane. Now that he knew that was something that had been a part of Davey long before he turned himself into a werewolf, he didn't feel much better. His empty stomach rolled at the memories he'd witnessed.

"So that's who you talked about in your sleep," Spike said quietly. "You have someone out there in the forest, looking for you."

"Until Davey gets his bloody wank spanners on her," Blaze grunted in a flat tone.

Korban growled, catching Blaze's drift, even if he didn't quite understand. "He won't. He thinks he can outsmart her, and he's wrong. If he keeps underestimating her he'll soon find out exactly what she's capable of," he paused, tried not to lose his temper. Right now he had to try to keep calm and not give Davey what he wanted. The moment he lost control Davey would gain the upper hand.

"Maybe she found my brother and my pack," Hati added softly.

Hope filled Korban once more and just in time, as the doors opened and Davey returned, this time with a medical kit in his hands. The hum of electricity filled the air as the fluorescent lights flickered to life above them. "While they set up the traps, I think it's about time we play another game, one we can't play when they're around." Davey hauled the metal kit over to the center of the room, to the space between where their cages were circled. He set it down and opened it up with a metallic clank. "After all, it's been a little while since my wolves had a chance to really stretch their legs."

"You just proved your point that you're able to control the others, and that they're faster and stronger together than I am," Korban growled at him, and stopped pacing. "Enough with these games! I don't know what you really want to accomplish here, Davey, but if it's a fight you want you already got it! Let me out of this cage and we'll handle our business like men!"

"But that's just it, Korban." Davey rummaged through the kit, a sadistic grin spreading across his face as he pulled out a shiny scalpel, studying it closely for a moment, then setting it back down into the box. "We aren't men." He began to rummage through the box again. "You and I aren't all that different, but you're definitely not what I expected Korban. I saw that. You lost your mother when you were young like I did. Lucky you though, no Daddy or Daddy's belt in your life. Also lucky to be in the right place, the right time, to rescue sweet little Sophie. She's quite a catch for someone like you. Someone... soft."

His eyebrows raised and his grin widened as he picked up a yellow plastic tube with a bright orange cap on one end and a blue tip on the other. For a moment Korban thought it was a marker, but then he recognized it from when RJ was studying for his first aid course. An EpiPen, which was an adrenaline injection often used to counteract an allergic reaction.

Davey pulled out three more, then closed up the box and set the three on top. He got to his feet and walked over to Spike's cage. The burly werewolf was trembling as Davey approached, tapping the side of the plastic pen against his palm. "It's a shame how attached you are to her, Korban, and how attached she is to you. Clearly when I find her, if you're still around, it'll be impossible to have her for myself. So I guess that leaves me with no other choice… as fun as it would be to wait and face off with you on a full moon night… I think you've outlived your usefulness."

Korban felt a chill rush through him, and found himself at a loss for words.

"I could just put a silver bullet in you, but that's not too sporting, and it would be too quick and not so much fun. You deserve at least one final chance to prove yourself, especially since you're the first one I've met with eyes like mine. And really, you've entertained me, so at least there's that," Davey smiled and pulled his keys from his pocket.

"What… what is it you're going to do to me?" Korban fumbled, his heart in his throat despite himself. He tried to play it cool, but he'd seen what Davey was capable of doing, and now he was talking so casually about killing him off.

"Well, I can't control you as easily as the others, otherwise I maybe wouldn't have to do this. We'll never know for sure." Davey opened up Spike's cage, and beckoned him over with his free hand while he wielded the injection at the ready in his other one. The large werewolf whimpered and reluctantly moved toward him, holding out his shaking arm. "You see, Korban, I can control my wolves, like you saw before, but as men they're still… able to fight me in some things.

As wolves though… well… I have complete control over them. They're nothing more than big ol' lap dogs for Davey. But waiting for the full moon, well that's also not so much fun. So I had to get a little creative, in order to help inspire my boys. That's where this little baby comes in." He waved the EpiPen and then patted Spike on the arm. "Observe, and learn."

Without further warning, Davey snapped the pen into Spike's arm. The overweight werewolf yelped out and cradled his arm, and began shaking as the adrenaline was injected into his body. Davey took a step back and opened up the cage. "Please, Davey, no, Davey!" Spike whimpered, but the yellow-eyed werewolf only laughed.

"Here, Spikey… shift. Turn for me." Davey's eyes seemed to glow a little at the command, and the larger man whimpered and fell to his knees.

Korban watched in horror as Spike began to shake harder and curled into fetal position on the floor of his cage. He whined, a half-human, half-animal sound and began to writhe on the ground in agony. Spike's hands frantically clutched at his own chest, his face scarlet as he gasped for air. "Stop it! You're killing him!"

Korban could hear Spike's heartbeat, racing even faster than his own. The large man was flopping on the ground like a fish, moaning and whimpering as his skin began to ripple, and bones began to bend and stretch. He hadn't seen someone transform like this since Sophie had been injected with that dark serum, and he watched in horror as the transformation began to take hold over the massive man.

The wolf wasn't meant to be summoned without the full moon, and seemed to be fighting against the change. Davey only stepped over Spike's twitching body and headed over to Blaze's cage, only pausing to bend down and pick up a second pen on his way over. "It won't kill Spike, well, it hasn't so far anyway. On to the second round! Blaze… my lovely Blaze. Wait until you see his wolf. Magnificent. Not as big as our big boy Spike, but it's hard to beat a man with as much mass as good ol' Spikey. I actually had to help my brother and Jimmy get him out of the pit, you know." He used his key on Blaze's cage then opened the door. "Your turn, Blaze. Come here, now."

The British werewolf grumbled but obeyed, though his gaze remained focused on the floor. "Arm," Davey commanded, and Blaze held out his arm. He winced when Davey injected him, and gritted his teeth as he sank to his knees and began to transform as well.

Korban watched as dark brown and black fur began to sprout from Spike's body, and Blaze grunted and stifled a moan as his body began to twist and transform. Davey left Blaze's cage open and he headed over to Hati's cage. He had to try to stall him, to stop him from doing this. "What will this achieve? Why are you tormenting them like this?"

"I'm freeing them, Korban." Davey scooped up another adrenaline injection as he explained. "They are my wolves. My pack. When they're finished transforming they'll do exactly as I say. You'll be nothing more than meat to them. But we'll make it a fair fight. I'll let you choose as a courtesy. If you want to join them as a wolf, too... or if you think you can handle them as a man."

The thought of being forced to turn again without the full moon made his already chilled blood run even colder. To be stuck as a wolf, and potentially be more influenced by Davey as a result, brought a whole new set of fears into his mind. If Davey kept him stuck as a wolf, and he was lucky enough to catch Sophie... he didn't want to think about the possibilities. "I'll... I'll stay human."

"Aww, what a shame," Davey frowned as he unlocked Hati's cage and whistled sharply to him. "Over here. Now, Hati."

Hati hesitated, as long as he could, but when Davey glared at him he stumbled forward towards the door. Spike was panting, fully transformed into the largest werewolf that Korban had ever seen, his markings and build similar to that of a giant Rottweiler dog. Across the way from him Blaze finished his transformation, the British werewolf a solid, snowy white color. He stumbled a little from his cage then splayed out on the ground away from his cage on his belly.

"This is only Hati's second time playing this game, but I'm sure he'll play it well. Give me your arm." Davey ordered, and Hati struggled for a moment, but inevitably lifted his arm. "Good boy."

The doors suddenly opened, which drew everyone's attention to the entrance. For a moment, Korban hoped the Calvary had arrived. To his growing disappointment, it was only Jimmy and Earl returning. "We got the traps reset, Davey, but we didn't find the girl."

Relief lightened the growing anxiety that had begun to take root inside Korban. They didn't have Sophie. She was safe for now.

"Damn, well, at least I have a little more time to prepare. And dispose of Korban's body." Davey licked his lips, which made a fresh wave of nausea turn his stomach.

"Body disposal?" Earl seemed to pale at the words as much as Korban did. "He seems rather alive to me."

"For the moment," Davey purred, and then gestured to his wolves on the ground. "Stand guard by the door, sit back and get your camera ready to record this. I'm in complete control here. We're going to have the standoff of the century. Korban here is going to prove himself, man versus wolf pack. If he can defeat all my wolves… then I think it's only fair to let him go."

Now he wanted him to kill the others to earn his freedom, all while he filmed it? He didn't trust Davey; he'd seen his temper at work. It made his own anger look like embers compared to a flame thrower. He wouldn't kill the others; he had to come up with a different way to stop them from attacking him. "It's not too late, we can still talk about this, Davey," Korban tried, but at that, Davey rolled his eyes and jammed the injection into Hati's arm.

Unlike Spike and Blaze, though, Hati didn't remain as quiet as he crumpled to the ground and the transformation began to take hold. As his body began to shake the young man gave a loud, low moan of agony that quickly turned into an even louder, bellowing scream that echoed through the building. The screams only escalated into howls as the transformation began, bones breaking and skin shifting, tan fur sprouting free and growing to cover his contorted body.

Davey turned to face Korban, delighted, as Spike padded timidly over to him, and Blaze joined him at his side. Hati, a light tan colored werewolf, still howled and thrashed on the floor, but would soon be by his side as well. Spike and Blaze tilted their heads back and joined in Hati's howling, the trio's song a haunting sound that echoed through the barn.

Davey gave Korban a victorious grin. "You're sure you still want to face my pack as a man Korban?"

~*~

"You should go back." Valkyrie and Odin had been quietly arguing for the last few minutes now, which had halted their plan of attack. Sophie paced anxiously, and Freki had joined her. "We can't leave the kids defenseless. If something happens to me—"

"They need their mother, Val, you should go back, and I can handle the front lines here. They have guns, and if they start shooting, I want you as far away as..."

A mournful, pained howl interrupted their argument. Sophie froze and turned her gaze back to the barn. "How... how is that possible? It's not even close to the full moon," Val gawked at the sound in disbelief.

Sophie rubbed her arms, a chill suddenly in the air. "It's possible to turn without the moon, but..." Her voice trailed off as the howl grew louder, more pained.

Next to her Freki tensed. "That's Hati!" Skoll exclaimed, and Geri caught him by the arm as he lunged toward the sound.

"Wait a minute, wait a minute!" Geri struggled to hold him back, and Odin caught his other arm.

Skoll growled in frustration. "Let me go! I need to go help him!"

"We're going to go help him! We need to go in there with a plan!" Odin chastised him.

Skoll struggled for another moment against them, despite their words, and Val went over, put her hand on his shoulder. She opened her mouth to speak to him when suddenly some more howls joined Hati's. Sophie's heart skipped a beat. The time for planning was over. Something was happening in that barn, and time was up.

"We don't have time for this!" Sophie snapped at them. "We can plan all day and it won't be enough to cover all the ins and outs! We need to go in there now, before it's too late!"

"We can't just burst in there without some sort of plan!" Val hissed as her eyes narrowed in frustration.

"We know there's two armed men, and," Freki sniffed the air, "at least two, no, three werewolves besides Hati and Korban in there. That I can scent out anyway."

"We need to go help them now!" Skoll insisted, panic in his eyes. "That's definitely my brother, he's in trouble, and we need to get to him now!"

The howling stopped, and with it, Sophie's heart sank again. A strange, tense quiet fell around them in the absence of the haunting sound. She didn't know if one of those howls belonged to Korban, but she wasn't going to stand around out here waiting any longer. She looked to Freki, then the others. "They said he wants me. They set those traps trying to capture me. I can go in there and play bait. While they're distracted, you all go in and get Korban and Hati out of there."

Val frowned. "What about you? If you're the bait they could capture you too!"

"I won't let that happen," Sophie vowed, and started towards the barn. As she strode forward, an idea bubbled into her head, and while it was risky, a plan was born. She glanced over her shoulder to the others. "Let's get our guys back."

16: BRAWL

Davey had won. The triumphant smirk on his face didn't seem to be fading away any time soon. He approached Korban's cage, giving the keys a happy jingle. He chuckled, held up a hand. "Stay, boys. Let's give him a chance to step out of his cage. I don't need all of you getting burned by silver."

Korban's heart was in his throat. Facing not one, but three werewolves didn't give him the best odds. He wasn't sure he'd do much better as a wolf. Time was running out, and Davey hummed some familiar tune under his breath as he unlocked Korban's cage. He wasn't sure he could find his voice to plead for his own life. He wasn't even sure it would make a difference if he could talk at the moment. Davey's twisted mind was already set on destroying him. It would take a miracle to change it now.

The lock clicked open and Davey stepped back with a dramatic flourish, that mocking grin accompanied by a mocking bow, his yellow eyes never leaving Korban. "Come out and play, Korban."

His hands curled into fists. He couldn't succumb to his fear now. He wouldn't give this monster the satisfaction of killing him while he begged for his life. He could hone in on his anger, and hope that in the end he wouldn't simply cave in to the tears that threatened to fall. He tried to focus not on his fear but his frustration. He turned his own trademark smile on full blast as he walked stiffly but confidently out of the cage. Something about meeting the other werewolf's grin must have unnerved him, and for a moment Davey's arrogant look wavered. He really wasn't used to being challenged, and at least Korban could do that. "My, aren't we confident?" Davey purred as he recovered and bared his teeth again.

Korban met his challenge, fueled by his own inner fire. No longer stuck in the silver cage, and despite being literally surrounded by wolves, he was on the same ground level as Davey. And no matter what happened next, he wasn't going to go down as this cocky bastard's bitch. "Yeah, actually," he began, circling around Davey, though the cages blocked most of his escape routes, especially with three werewolves flanking him. A quick glance at the door evoked a nasty frown from Earl who held a small camcorder, and the loud metallic clack of Jimmy taking off the safety from his rifle. Good. If Davey wanted to make a show of his final moments, he'd put on one hell of a memorable performance. "You could kill me. You could have your brother and your bestie over there pump me full of silver. You could have Hati, Blaze, and Spike rip me to shreds. You could eat my liver with fava beans and wash it all down with a nice Chianti for all I care. Though I bet in your case it might be more like a Budweiser. But no matter what you do, no matter how hard you try to impress her, there's no way in hell you'll ever convince Sophie to be with you. Not in this lifetime, or any other lifetime. And do you know why?"

Davey's lip curled and his yellow eyes held a stormy look in them. "Why is that, Korban?" His voice was colder, and he knew he was getting under his skin.

He looked Davey right into his golden glare. "Because I'm the better man," Korban growled as he clenched his fists. "No matter what you do to end me, she chose to be with me. And nothing you or anyone else can do to me will ever change that. Because even if it wasn't for long, I loved the smartest, most beautiful and incredible woman. I didn't have to manipulate her or use some monster mojo to convince her to be with me. It was her choice, and together we were happy."

Davey's eyes narrowed and he squared his jaw. "So these are your last words? Declaring your love for your lady?" He burst into a manic fit of laughter. "Ah, delightful Korban. Amusing me all the way to the end. Should I have Earl zoom in for dramatic effect? Women like that, don't they? Shakespeare sonnets and shit." His look turned dark again, and just as quickly as it came the laughter faded away. "You think I care enough whether she will want to be with me or not? Of course, it'd be easier for her if she didn't resist. Think of your death as… just a stepping stone to making her life easier. Because if you're around, she'll want to fight me. I do like a good fight, that's true, but I have other plans for sweet Sophie." He licked his lips and made a lewd gesture with his tongue. "Maybe I'll just have my wolves play a little with you, and keep what's left of you around to see exactly what I have in store for her."

Korban let out a much more menacing growl this time. Davey leered and held up his hand, the three wolves perked their ears up and stiffened, awaiting his command.

Instead of a snap of his fingers, a sudden knock came at the door that made all eyes – both wolf and human alike – turned toward the entrance. Jimmy and Earl looked surprised and confused, turning to one another and then to Davey for instructions. Another polite rap at the door came and Davey waved his hand. "Well? What are you waiting for you idjits? We've got company. Answer it!"

The two human henchmen didn't look so sure at first, but Earl swallowed and lowered his camera, then turned the handle to open the door while Jimmy fixed the aim of his rifle from Korban to their mystery guest. Korban's racing heart skipped a beat as the door opened to reveal who had interrupted Davey's twisted game.

She stood there, an image he both dreamed and feared, but even Korban's jaw dropped in surprise at the sight of her. She wore form-fitting, faded blue jeans and a pair of black combat boots. Her black t-shirt was tied off at her midriff, revealing her smooth stomach. She held herself in a confident stance, her chin held high and shoulders straight. Her pale blue eyes searched the room and lit up when they landed on Korban. "There you are! You know, I've been looking everywhere for you, Korban!"

"Sophie!" Korban began to warn her as the conflicting feelings of relief and worry struck him at the same time, but he froze as Jimmy's gun clicked. Sophie didn't move, simply kept a demure smile on her face.

"Wait!" Davey snarled at him then smiled to her in return. "Put it down or you'll shoot her you idiot." He ran his hand through his hair, and stepped toward her. Jimmy flinched at Davey's look and lowered his weapon. "You'll have to excuse my friend. We don't get company around here too often." Korban took a step toward Davey to stop him from going near Sophie, but he waved a hand and the three wolves growled in unison and blocked him as they padded forward.

Sophie tilted her head a little, her blonde hair falling over her shoulder at the motion. "I suppose it would be difficult to have guests way out here. Pardon my manners, just barging in like this without even introducing myself. My name is Sophie. I should thank you for finding Korban for me."

"I'm Davey, that there's my brother Earl, and our old pal Jimmy. And I know exactly who you are, Sophie Bane," Davey purred, looking like the cat who swallowed the canary, or perhaps more accurately the wolf who swallowed a grandmother.

"Good," Sophie said and gestured towards Korban, "then you'll understand, Davey, that I'll be sure to compensate you and your friends handsomely for finding and taking care of Korban. I don't exactly have access to my bank account out here but I will be sure to reward you for his safe return."

Korban glanced from Sophie to Davey, then back to Sophie again. For a moment Davey seemed to actually consider it, but he chuckled and shook his head. "While I'm sure you could pay me, I'm a simple man with simple needs. Besides, I'm pretty sure that Korban is starting to like it here, aren't you, Korban?"

"Hardly," Korban began, and Blaze stepped closer to him with a low growl that made him take a step back, which evoked a growl from Hati and Spike.

Sophie's smile faded as Davey laughed again. "You came at a pretty good time. As you can see we're just in the middle of a game here, and you're just in time to be part of the audience."

"A game, huh? Sounds like fun. I'm not much into just standing by and watching, though. How do I play?" Sophie asked, giving her hair another playful toss back.

"So eager to join in on the fun! I like your spirit." Davey walked closer to Sophie and began to circle her. His eyes roamed up and down her body and he gave a low whistle under his breath. "You're even hotter in person."

Sophie glanced over to Korban as Davey's predatory gaze followed the curves of her body. Their eyes met and she gave him a meaningful, pointed look as she tried to relay some silent message. Just as quickly it was gone. Korban wasn't sure what it meant exactly, but he trusted her. He tried to swallow the lump in his throat again and remained as still as possible while the three wolves started to circle around him and mimic Davey's movements.

"I take care of myself, as best as I can." Sophie kept her voice level along with her gaze. As Davey stepped closer to her, Korban could see her tense. He was getting a little too close for comfort and Korban had to bite the inside of his cheek to keep from growling out.

"I can see that," he responded, then leered at her with another cold smile. "I like that."

Korban watched her, tried to warn her with a look of his own. His fists were clenched, his knuckles turned white. He had to get her away from Davey before it was too late. But how could he even get near that monster, when he had three closer problems of his own that closed in like sharks, their hungry eyes fixed on him?

~*~

She was buying time now, but so far it seemed to be working. All eyes were on her, save for the three wolves that surrounded Korban. She briefly wondered which one was Hati when she had arrived there, but didn't let her thoughts wander long. Korban was in danger, and even from where she stood she could smell the fear rolling off him and the anger targeted at his captor. He was wearing only a pair of dirty and blood-stained gray sweatpants and seemed thinner and gaunter than she remembered, his cheeks more hollowed and his ribs more visible. It pained her to see him this way. What had Davey and his henchmen been doing to him?

It took all her strength not to rush towards him and fight off the wolves around him. She kept her focus on Davey, careful to watch him but cautious to avoid direct contact with those yellow eyes. Though Korban had the same wolf-like eyes this werewolf's gaze seemed cold and creepy. She fought not to shudder as his eyes undressed her. "What else is it that you like, Davey?" Sophie asked. "If it's not money you want, what is it that moves you?"

"Like I said, the simple things." Davey reached out and she

suppressed the urge to flinch away as he ran his fingers through her hair, brushing back her blonde strands. "The basic pleasures a man can experience in life. Hunting, fishing, fighting." He paused, smiled to her, and caressed her cheek with his knuckles. His touch made her skin crawl and this time she couldn't help but step back away from him. "I'd like to add to that list, Sophie, but there aren't too many lovely ladies like yourself out here. Maybe we can come to an agreement… you give me what I want, and I'll release Korban."

She wanted to run. This close she could smell Davey's wolf, not that his eyes weren't a dead giveaway, but it wasn't like the safe smell of forest that accompanied Korban or even Valkyrie's pack. He reeked of something cold and harsh, undefinable, but it made her think of blood, pain, death. It made her sick to her stomach, and inside her sleeping wolf began to wake and also wanted to run away.

She steadied her nerves and focused instead on his human features: his square jaw, the fall of his brown hair over his forehead. He had the eyes of a predator but he was ruggedly handsome. It was a shame he was clearly some kind of psychopath or he would be more attractive. She could continue this game and buy more time until the cavalry arrived. She could smell his growing desire but it wasn't exactly aimed at her. Every time he glanced over to where he'd sent his wolves on Korban his cruel smirk widened, his eyes lit up, his pulse quickened. She realized that she was only a means to an end for him. He didn't get off on her exactly. He wanted to cause pain to Korban and to the others who were trapped there. He only hoped to add her to his collection.

She swallowed and found her voice again, "What is it you want?" This time she looked him in the eye, even though when she met his gaze she felt even more creeped out as the sensation of insects crawling over her skin returned.

This pleased him and he let his eyes roam over her body again, a dark look in those vibrant eyes. "I want you of course. Right here and now. Choose me, and I'll let him go." He gestured to Korban with a wave of his hand.

The wolves that paced around him began to growl again, their lips curled into vicious snarls. Korban gave a fearful look her way that spoke volumes. Sophie saw Davey's grin only grow and something inside her snapped. She kept a cool demeanor as she plastered a smile of her own across her face. "Right here and now, in front of all these guys?" She asked and lifted her finger to curl a few pale strands of her hair.

Davey's eyes went from Korban to her, and he nodded then licked his lips. "Mmm hmm."

"All right, but I don't think you'll be able to handle a woman like me," Sophie said and locked eyes with him, reaching up with one hand and touching the rough stubble on Davey's cheek with her smooth palm. She steeled herself for what she planned to do next as she closed the space between them and leaned in. This close there was no doubt he would sense it the way she could sense him and she relished the moment when realization hit him and his eyebrows raised in surprise, right before she curled her free hand into a fist and thrust as much power as she could into an uppercut aimed for his stomach.

The blow knocked the wind from his lungs in a rush that doubled him over. Before he could recover, she brought her knee crashing up into his face with a loud crack. He fell over with a grunt of pain, and curled into himself. His nose dripped blood onto the dirt floor and his shoulders tensed. He spat blood on the ground as he gasped to catch his breath.

She flexed her hand, her knuckles sore from the strike. Her heart pounded and the thrill of striking him down sent adrenaline through her, the rush pure satisfaction. "That was for Korban, you sick bastard," she snarled.

Davey's shoulders shook silently, and then a low, dark chuckle accompanied the movement. He lifted his yellow eyes to Sophie, intense lust reflected in his inhuman gaze. "Oh, I like this game even more than what I had planned for us! And when I'm done with you, sweet Sophie, I'm going to be sure to savor every minute I make you scream. I'll be sure to keep Korban around to enjoy the show." He turned his head to his wolves briefly as he stood. "If he makes a move to stop me, tear out his throat."

He lifted his fists and his eyes lit up with growing desire as he took a fighter's stance and closed in on Sophie. He spat more blood on the ground and a red drop trailed down the corner of his mouth. "You're definitely full of surprises. I like that. It'll be much more fun beating you down if you actually put up a real fight."

"Then let's get to it! I don't have all day to braid our hair and discuss our feelings." Sophie held up her fists and met his fighter's stance with one of her own, just in time as Davey launched his fist toward her. She blocked the blow with a sweeping motion of her arm, moving fast to block his next strike as their fight began.

~*~

Korban felt completely useless as Sophie began to take Davey on by herself. He wanted to go to her side and help her fight against him but the bared teeth that snapped at him were an effective barrier. Sophie was holding her own, but every time Davey got a hit in on her his own anger began to rise again. He had to get through this obstacle and join his Mate in battle.

It suddenly dawned on him. Davey's own words floated into his memory. He was like him. They both had the same yellow eyes. Maybe he could turn the tables after all. He forced his gaze away from Sophie and Davey's struggle, despite every ounce of his being that wanted to rush to her side. First things first. He met the eyes of Spike as he slunk by, hackles raised and teeth bared. The massive black and brown werewolf averted his gaze. Still submissive even now. Korban kept his body still and whispered to him, "Spike."

His dark ears perked in his direction, and he glanced his way, but didn't quite meet his eyes. "Spike," Korban tried again and made his name a command for attention. "Spike look at me."

The huge wolf hesitated for a moment, and then turned his head to look at him. Korban smiled, but Blaze and Hati snarled and snapped at him still. He had one, now for the other two. Sweat began to bead on his forehead as he glanced over to Hati. "Hati," he began, but suddenly a new commotion caught his attention.

"Oh yeah! Get her good brother!" Earl cheered as Davey knocked Sophie to the ground and pinned her beneath him.

Both Earl and Jimmy's attention were honed in on their boss as he wrestled Sophie's wrists and straddled her ribcage so she couldn't get a strike in with her legs. His heart went to his throat, and he cried out to her, "So–!"

His cry was immediately cut off as the door burst open again and four men and a woman he didn't recognize burst into the room. Two large men who looked like bikers – one a burly, long-haired blond and the other lean with dark curls – grabbed Earl, causing him to drop his camera. The others resembled bikers as well, clad in leather and denim with one guy wearing a camouflage bandana as they charged at Jimmy. The wiry human cried out in shock and protest and waved his gun.

Before anyone could make sense of the chaos, a gun shot went off and echoed in the silence that followed.

17: FORFEIT

Time seemed to stop the moment the shot went off. Sophie's heart went from racing in her chest to a sudden halt. The quiet was punctured by a low moan of pain, and to her horror Freki suddenly fell down to his knees as he clutched his stomach. Blood bubbled from his mouth as he yelped, "Ah, it burns!"

"Freki no!" Tears filled Sophie's eyes as he collapsed.

Skoll snarled and knocked the still smoking rifle from Jimmy's hands and then pinned him to the wall by his throat. Val rushed over to Freki's side and began to bark orders. "Odin and Skoll, keep them pinned, Geri get his gun away from him."

Geri snarled as he yanked the holstered shotgun away as Odin restrained Earl. He snapped the safety back on and bent the barrel of the gun with his hands before he chucked it across the room. "Done."

"Geri, come here and help me with your brother," Valkyrie knelt down alongside Freki as she applied pressure to the bloody wound in his chest.

He moaned in pain as the color drained from him, his face was twisted in agony. His breath came out in short, shallow gasps. "Hurts, it burns," Freki moaned between breaths.

Sophie continued to struggle and tried to free herself from Davey, but watched helplessly as Freki shuddered and coughed. His eyes rolled into the back of his head and he went still. Her heart broke as his hand went limp and flopped to the ground.

A furry blur rushed past and one of the wolves that had paced around Korban was suddenly at Freki's side. Val blinked in surprise and touched his tan fur as she blinked tears from her eyes. "Hati?"

The wolf whimpered then nudged Freki's pale hand. He tossed his head back and let loose a mournful howl for his fallen pack mate.

"Silver bullets," Davey said and started to chuckle, and Sophie punched him across his jaw while he was distracted.

"Heartless monster!" Sophie sneered at him, tears in her eyes.

He growled and caught her fist before she could strike him again. Davey glared up at the intruders as he flexed his jaw. "Who the hell are you people anyway?" he demanded, then angrily grabbed Sophie by her throat while she blinked tears from her eyes and began to choke off her air. "How dare you interrupt my fun! Nobody move or I'll kill her! I'm the one in charge here and I want answers!"

Sophie's vision swam and she grabbed at his hands, tried to pry them away from her throat. She clawed at his wrists and writhed against him. Dark spots began to appear before her eyes when a pair of growls came from close by. Too close. Davey's grip tightened.

"Let her go, Davey, or you're wolf kibble," Korban's voice commanded, echoed by a duo of vicious snarls.

Davey's face reddened. His rage made his hands shake, and suddenly go slack. Sophie gasped, choked on the fresh air entering her lungs. "Impossible." Davey breathed in surprise, and Sophie turned her gaze from where Freki fell to where Korban stood.

Her Mate stood there like a heroic vision. His eyes glistened like molten gold, and flanked at his sides were two of the wolves that had circled him like hungry sharks before, their gaze now focused on Davey. "Get your hands off her and move away, or you're going to find out what it's like to be the main course."

For a moment Davey's entire body tensed, and he glared at Korban in challenge, but when the massive black and brown wolf stepped forward and licked his chops, he got up on his feet quickly, holding his hands up defensively. "Okay, okay Korban. Well played. Good game."

Sophie sat up, coughed and sputtered to catch her breath, her hand going to her throat to rub it. Korban moved alongside her and offered her a hand up as he kept his eyes on Davey. Still light-headed, it felt like a dream until she took his warm hand in hers. "Korban," she whispered his name, her throat still raw from being choked, "my Korban."

He pulled her up to her feet and she flung her arms around him. She couldn't hold back the tears as she clung to him, buried her nose into his throat and breathed in his scent as he held her just as fiercely. Pine, forest, animal fur and musk. Home. The familiar scent, peppered with sweat, dirt, remnants of pain and relief, but even more than that she could smell his power. Strong but gentle, it added some spice to the air and filled her heart. He was solid and real in her arms again at last. She wouldn't lose the chance to tell him now. "I love you Korban," she confessed into his ear.

"I know," he murmured in return, "I love you too Sophie." He squeezed her tightly in his arms as a wild and warm fragrance radiated from him now, his power enhanced by her words and his bond with the wolves.

The two wolves stepped ahead of him and toward their quarry. Davey kept his hands up and glanced to his two human comrades for help, but Odin and Skoll kept them firmly pinned to the wall. He narrowed his eyes and his eyes lit up a little; the feeling of ants crawling on her skin made Sophie turn around and Korban growled at him again. "No. Your game is over, Davey." He kept an arm around Sophie as he stepped forward. "I told you I'm the better man. You didn't see that I'm also the better wolf. You brought nothing but pain, hunger, loneliness, and fear to them. These wolves will never follow you again."

The white wolf's dark lips curled back and those sharp teeth snapped at him, caused Davey to take several steps back. The gigantic dark-furred wolf lunged and Davey reeled backwards, until he found himself in the cage that smelled of Korban. His eyes widened in realization but Korban moved closer, Sophie at his side, and he slammed the cage door on him. This time the metallic clang held a far more satisfying sound.

"What should we do with these two?" Skoll growled out as Jimmy continued to flail against him.

"Lock them up. Let them see how it feels for a while," Korban suggested.

"Good idea," Skoll smiled, yanked Jimmy away from the wall and shoved him towards an empty cage.

Odin dragged a protesting Earl over to a cage of his own and they snapped the cages shut. "Where are the keys?" he asked.

Sophie smirked pointedly to Davey as she revealed what she'd slipped from his pocket during their tussle. She gave the keys a taunting rattle and watched as Davey's surprise turned once again to rage as he realized he'd been truly defeated. "Don't worry, you're not going anywhere." She kept her eyes on Davey the entire time she locked his cage, then tossed the keys over to Odin, who was happy to secure the two other cages.

Her attention moved back to Freki now that the threat had been contained. She took Korban by the hand and led him over to the others, his warm hand a welcome comfort after missing him for so long. She wasn't sure she would ever let him out of her sight anytime soon if she could help it. "Freki, is he…?"

"His heartbeat is slowing down," Val somberly reported. "It won't be much longer now, but… I don't think he's in pain. He's lost consciousness at least."

Sophie turned her head away and buried her face into Korban's shoulder, her heart broken. He wrapped his arms around her again and held her close. "I'm so sorry," Korban said softly to her and to everyone gathered there.

"Let's get him outside, out of here." Odin said and bent down to help scoop his body up. "We'll try to get him home while there's time. He shouldn't spend his last minutes in this dungeon."

Geri helped Odin lift Freki carefully from the ground and they headed out the door. Val stood up, stared at Freki's blood that dripped from her hands. "This isn't how it was supposed to end," she shook her head solemnly. "We're supposed to go home as a pack."

Hati whimpered, his tail curled beneath him to his stomach. "Let's go." Val turned and headed for the door.

"Wait! You're just going to leave us here, like this?" Earl asked in a panic.

"Don't worry, guys," Korban said as the others headed outside. "Lucky for you I am a nicer guy. I won't leave you here to starve and rot. I'll be calling the authorities," he said, then paused and smiled, his arm around Sophie as he gave one last look to Davey and his minions, "and I'm sure they'll be on their way to pick you all up in a day or so. Whenever we make it home I'll be making the call. Until then maybe you should sit and think about what you've done."

"He's joking, he won't leave us here, not like this," Davey chuckled, but his laughter faded as they turned and headed out the door. "Korban's a good guy; he won't just abandon us like this. He's better than that."

"Korban is a good guy," Sophie said, stopping at the exit to reach for the lights, "but I'm not. Not after what you put him through, and your silver bullet ending another really good man."

She clicked off the lights, and squeezed Korban's hand. "Let's go home."

They ignored the swearing, bellowed protests, and the howl of rage that came as they closed the door and headed around the corner towards the exit, the two wolves silent sentries at their side.

18: GAME OVER

The sun had started to sink behind the mountains once more as they stepped out into the twilight together. Korban breathed in the mountain air deeply in a long, shuddering breath. The sky was clear, a beautiful pink and lavender that faded into a dark violet. Stars began to twinkle and a sliver of moonlight revealed a growing crescent moon. He stared up at it and felt a new appreciation for his favorite time of the month, and another reason to celebrate it now.

Sophie kept her hand in his, and put her head against his shoulder as they walked outside. Their fingers intertwined, he leaned over and breathed in the scent of her hair. This wasn't a dream, this was real. He was free at last. Sophie had saved him with a little help from her friends.

Spike brushed against his leg as they walked toward the others, and he reached down with his free hand to touch his dark fur. The massive wolf's shoulder came up to his hip and his muscles sang with tension. Power. He still felt his own strength, like some invisible lead that connected him to Spike and Blaze, and even more loosely Hati nearby. Now that things were quiet, he had a new dilemma to face. How were they supposed to turn back to normal since they'd been forced to transform? Still, as Spike whimpered at his side he wondered how he could help them now. Worse yet, what if he couldn't help them and they were stuck like this? He couldn't let that happen. He wouldn't let Davey ruin the rest of these men's lives.

He stopped and both Spike and Blaze paused and looked to him, waiting obediently for a command. He looked to Sophie who smiled to him and squeezed his hand again. He could do this.

With his free hand he reached again for Spike, ran his hand over his thick, dark mane of fur. His fingers trembled a little, but not from fear. He took a deep breath in, his eyes locked with Spike's. "Spike," he said his name like a command. "It's okay now. We're going home." He glanced to Blaze. "Blaze, it's safe now. You both can rest, until the moon is full again."

The two wolves stood there for a moment in the quiet of the forest, the night song beginning to play again as crickets chirped in the reeds nearby. An owl hooted from the safety of a tree many yards away. Then a soft whimper came, and Spike's body tensed then shuddered. Korban and Sophie looked on; it was strange to watch the wolf vanish, the fur recede into the skin as bones and muscle melted back into its human shape.

After a few minutes, instead of a massive wolf being by their side, a large, naked hairy man with long, dark hair and a full beard knelt and shivered. He blinked in confusion for a moment, fear in his eyes as he glanced around, disoriented. He looked up to Korban and the fear melted away as he spoke, his voice hoarse but heavy with relief, "Korban?"

He nodded, and the big fellow's eyes darted around anxiously. "Is, is D-Davey still around here?"

"We locked him up in there, he's not going anywhere except prison," Korban said, then reached out and patted his shaking shoulder. "He's not going to hurt you ever again. Not if I have a say in it."

Spike's eyes filled with tears. "He's r-really… he's the one that's t-trapped in a cage now?"

"Karma's a bitch, like me when someone decides to cross those I love," Sophie said, and smiled gently to him, "I'll see if I can find you guys something to cover up with while we head back to camp."

"Th-thank you," Spike stammered. He wrapped his arms around himself and glanced around the clearing anxiously.

The white wolf completed his transformation and Korban offered him a hand up. "Thank you doesn't even begin to cover it," Blaze said crisply, accepting his hand and standing up. He brushed the dirt from his pale skin. "Where's this camp of yours?"

"It's maybe a mile or so away from here," Sophie said.

"Well, if I may be blunt, I'd much rather be as far from this place stark naked than to bring anything with that monster's scent on it anywhere near my person, ever again," Blaze said, sniffing the air.

Spike nodded in agreement. "W-what he s-said."

"Okay. Let's keep moving then," Sophie said as they turned and headed toward the forest where the others had headed.

Spike shivered as he walked, and would stop and glance back periodically, as though afraid they were being followed. Korban stayed at his side as they met up with the rest of Hati's pack. "I got these guys back to normal; it's your turn Hati if you like."

The tan wolf slunk over to him with his head hung low, a dejected look in his eyes. The blond man and woman looked to one another, their expressions lined with grief. Korban blinked in surprise. "You've got the same eyes as me, too."

She smiled grimly. "I guess we're the lucky ones, to stand out the way we do. You must be Korban. Sophie's told us a lot about you."

Korban grinned and blushed a little. Sophie gestured to the pack and as they walked she introduced everyone. "Korban, this is Valkyrie, Odin, Geri, Skoll and…" Her voice trailed off when she laid eyes on the man who'd been shot. "Freki. He was… is my friend," she corrected when she could still hear his heartbeat, though slow and strained, in his chest.

She frowned, remembering how bad the silver burned her when she simply touched the picture frame on Lucas's desk. As painful as it was, she couldn't imagine being shot with a silver bullet. It would be agonizing, and the thought of what Freki was going through made her heart ache. Still something nagged her. The pain would be incredible if the silver bullet was still in there. The bullet…

"Wait, stop!" Sophie said suddenly, a fleeting hope filled her. "The silver bullet, we have to get it out. It's killing him!" She looked to Val. "If we get it out, maybe he can heal. Maybe we can save him!"

"It's worth a shot," Geri agreed, looked to the others. "Not like any one of us is a doctor, but not like it matters either way. It's a chance, let's do it. It's what Freki would want. Just a chance."

"He's still fighting," Sophie said.

Blaze looked to the group. "I could try. I'm no surgeon but I was trained as a medic. I can get it out of him. Does anyone have a knife on them?"

"Sure, I do," Geri said, then retrieved a pocket knife from his pants and handed it to him.

They lowered Freki onto the ground between a circle of trees and stepped back to give Blaze room while he cut open Freki's bloody shirt to examine the wound. The bleeding had started to slow, but his blood was everywhere, including all over most of his pack mates. He'd lost so much blood that only a little more seemed to spring up as Blaze used the blade to pry into the bullet wound.

Spike winced and turned away, looking back to the barn. Korban gently patted his shoulder to comfort him. "Don't worry; they're locked up in there. Sophie's got the keys, and we'll turn them over to the police as soon as we get home."

"The p-police? I c-can't, I mean, they'll put us in qu-quarantine if we go to them! For what we've d-done!" Spike looked panicked.

"I have a friend with an open mind on the force, and when we get back to Syracuse, I promise it will be okay. They'll lock Davey and the others up for good. He won't hurt anyone else ever again," Korban reassured him.

Spike chewed on his bottom lip and didn't look so confident in his words, but it would take time. Korban gently patted him again, and then turned his attention to Hati, whose ears had perked up since Blaze began to remove the bullet from Freki's chest. "Let's get you back on two legs again buddy," Korban said with a smile then reached for Hati and concentrated, his eyes locked with Hati. "Hati, come back to us. Come back to your pack."

The tan wolf whimpered and then began to shift back. Hati panted and groaned, and soon was himself again. He coughed and shook his head, for a moment disoriented like Blaze and Spike had been, and then his eyes fixed on Korban again. He gave a lop-sided grin as he got up on his feet. He pulled Korban into a hug. "Thanks to you, buddy."

Korban hugged him back. "You're welcome Hati."

"Seriously, Korban. You saved my life and got us the hell out of... well, hell." Hati clapped his shoulder as he stepped back, and then firmly shook Korban's hand. "I'd say I owe you one, but well, I owe you a lot more than that, brother."

"If you guys can give us a ride home, believe me, we can call it even," Korban said.

"I got it!" Blaze exclaimed as he carefully pried out the bullet from Freki's chest.

They gathered around, watching as Blaze used the knife and his finger to pry the bullet from Freki. The small metal piece and his hands were slick with blood. Yet he didn't flinch, didn't yelp, and Sophie's vision filled with tears of relief. "It wasn't silver; the bullet he used wasn't silver."

"Well I'll be damned," Geri exhaled with a low whistle and shook his head in wonder as Freki suddenly moaned and began to cough and wheeze.

"Ahhh, oww," Freki groaned weakly as Geri embraced his brother.

Blaze turned to the others and held up the blood-soaked bullet carefully between his fingers. "He'll need to rest, but I can already hear his heartbeat getting stronger. The bullet was probably restricting blood flow, but it's not silver. He wouldn't be healing if it was and Sophie's right, I wouldn't even be able to touch this if it was the real thing."

"Davey said it was silver but he enjoyed mind games. Maybe he led us all on." Korban had never felt so relieved that Davey had lied.

"You lucky bastard, you gave us all quite a scare," Geri said, growling at his brother, but he couldn't hide the relief in his eyes. "Let's get him back to camp and get the hell out of here."

Skoll nodded. He helped Geri get Freki up and resumed carrying him again.

"As for that ride home, consider it done, friend. We're packing up camp and getting the hell out of dodge as soon as we can," Odin said, and went over to Val's side and took her hand in his. "I want my pack and my family as far away from this nightmare as possible. We can drop you two off in Syracuse, not a problem." He glanced to Spike and Blaze. "What about you guys? Where are you headed?"

"I'm going to head back to my camp to get my things and get on the next flight I can back to London," Blaze said. "I think I've spent enough time on holiday here."

Korban grinned. "So the British werewolf in New York is headed home?"

"I've had quite enough torture while here in America, enough to last me a lifetime. Please don't add terrible jokes to the long list of complaints I'll be surely sending to the embassy." Blaze groaned, and then smirked despite himself. "What about you, Spike?"

Spike glanced back nervously again, still fidgeting and anxious. Clearly it would be some time before he felt safe again. "I... I can't go back!" He yelped and suddenly lunged for Sophie. "I can't leave him like this!"

She cried out in surprise as he grabbed her by the arm, yanked the keys from her pocket, and began to race back towards the barn.

Korban's eyes went round in horror as he realized what he was doing. "He's going to free Davey!"

19: SYNDROME

Spike streaked across the clearing as fast as he could. He was almost to the barn door when Korban and Blaze caught up to him and grabbed him by his beefy arms. The large man flailed and struggled to free himself from them. "Let me go! Please! I'm doing this for all of us!" He was hysterical. His breathing was labored and his eyes were wide, round, and darting around fearfully. "If we let him go now he'll forgive us, he won't be angry for long, you'll see!"

"No! You are not letting that madman on the loose again! Not as long as I'm on American soil!" Blaze growled.

"Please! If we let him go, he'll forgive us! If we keep him trapped in there, and the police come... we can't let them take him away!" Spike began to wheeze and hyperventilate. "They'll put him in quarantine; they'll never let him go! You know what it's like in there! We can't do that to him!"

Pure panic and fear rolled off him like thick, choking cologne. Korban glanced from Spike to Blaze. "What's wrong with him?"

"I haven't got any bloody idea," Blaze grunted as Spike continued to writhe against him. "He's gone completely nutters. I thought if anyone would want to get the 'ell away from here it would be him. Davey used to beat him terribly if he so much as looked away when he was giving him an order. He was extra cruel to him; you saw how he would go on about his weight, mate. He was even worse to him before you showed up."

Korban struggled to get the keys from Spike, but he clutched them tight in his fist. "Spike! Listen to me! Take a deep breath."

"We need to let him free! It's not right to leave him like this!" Spike said, and began to sob.

He had to calm him down and stop him from freeing Davey. There wasn't much choice left but to try to use his power again. "Spike!" He barked his name like an order, and the larger man jumped as if he'd struck him.

Korban winced. He didn't want to force someone to do things against their will like Davey. He kept his gaze on Spike now that those fearful eyes were on his, and he said again, but in a gentler, still dominant tone, "Spike, you need to calm down. Take a breath."

The large man trembled, but kept his gaze on Korban. Once again he felt that odd floating sensation, but this time it didn't yank him from his body. Images flashed in front of him from Spike's past. He witnessed as he spent summers up in the Adirondacks at his camp for years, hunting and fishing. He was known as a gentle giant by those who knew him, a good guy with a lot of friends who would join him on his trips. Then one year he was attacked by a dark brown werewolf during a full moon night.

He spent time in quarantine, restrained to a clean, white hospital bed. Korban's stomach felt queasy as he watched the endless circle of white lab coats poke and prod him. Until one day, when his father, a man who resembled him but with more salt and pepper in his beard, showed up and told him he was going to be his sponsor. He felt an all too familiar relief flow through him as he was able to return home.

Things seemed to be going well for Spike. To celebrate his freedom, his father took him on a hunting trip to the Adirondacks once again later that month, for old time's sake. Only that night during the full moon Spike had been caught in one of Davey's wolf pits, and Davey had recovered him the next day.

Unlike the time he'd spent in Davey's mind, it was more like watching the scenes on a screen in front of him. They weren't as high definition, but they were informative. He shook his head suddenly, and blinked, looking at Spike in a new light. The larger man seemed calmer and in a daze.

"Steven," Korban said to him now, and Spike's eyes went round in surprise. "You aren't Spike. Davey called you that, but your true name is Steven Edson. You don't have to go to him. He doesn't own you. Your father has probably been worried sick looking for you all this time, if he's not in jail himself. He was your sponsor, right? Like my best friend RJ is mine." He patted Spike's – Steven's – arm. "He needs you like you needed him. You don't owe Davey anything after what he did to you."

"But the police..." Spike protested weakly and trailed off as his lower lip trembled uncontrollably. His eyes still held a glint of fear.

"He will serve his time, they'll put him in quarantine, and maybe he'll get a sponsor who can help rehabilitate him." Korban hoped not, and after what he'd witnessed he doubted that Davey was ever going to breathe free air again once he was locked away. But he was okay with that. For now, he had to soothe Steven's worries and get him away from that monster before he fell back into Davey's hands. "You did what you had to in order to survive, Steven. You became Davey's obedient Spike. You aren't that man or wolf. You are Steven Edson, and your father is out there waiting for you buddy. Let's get you back to him, okay?"

Tears welled in his eyes, and he handed Korban the keys as his hand uncontrollably shook and rattled them. "Please help me, Korban. I just... I just want to go home."

"Okay, big guy," Korban said, and gently cuffed him into a hug. "Let's all go home."

With Blaze on one side of him and Korban on the other, Steven headed back into the forest, away from the barn and Davey's hold on him. This time he didn't look back.

~*~

When they arrived at Val and Odin's camp it was around nine o' clock at night, and even as exhausted as they were they began to pack up the campsite. Blaze accompanied them on their way to make sure Spike didn't turn and run back. Thankfully, it seemed that moment had passed.

Val made sure everyone had clothes, sandwiches, and a beer in their hands to have something in their system before they began to clean up and prepare to leave. Korban lingered by the edge of the site, sitting next to Blaze on a fallen log. "Are you sure we can't talk you into hitching a ride with us?" he asked.

"I appreciate it, mate, but I'm afraid I'm more of a lone wolf, of sorts." Blaze watched the others and Korban could swear he saw a glimpse of longing in the British man's eyes. Still, he kept that stereotypical stiff upper lip when he met Korban's gaze. "Thank you, Korban, for everything you did in there. We wouldn't be free again without you. You and Sophie, and these wolves." He chuckled, shook his head. "So many wolves in the mountains. To think I thought it would be nothing but peace and quiet out here."

"So you came all the way from London to here for a vacation? I know the Adirondacks are beautiful but I'm surprised. A long airplane ride seems like it would be hell as a werewolf; I can barely stand to take a bus sometimes," Korban said, and wrinkled his nose. "It's going to be a long ride home, but I'm actually looking forward to it, for once."

Blaze chuckled. "It's a right test of your control, but if you travel during the right time of the month, it's not so bad. My advice? Take a holiday during a new moon, while your wolf is taking a nap, mate."

"I'll have to remember that," Korban grinned.

Blaze went quiet for a moment before he turned to him, a serious look in his eyes. "I came here for work, not for leisure. A foolish, personal journey," he began, then took a deep breath and continued. "I was working on a case. A string of murders in London. We thought maybe we'd had a Ripper copycat on our hands. It happens from time to time, but this time it was different. I followed the clues, but this wasn't your average serial killer. Turns out he was a werewolf, and I didn't know it until it was too late." He paused and frowned. "I tracked him down for two years. Over in London the rules are a bit stricter, the quarantine's much more… difficult to get out of. I spent the entire month before my first full moon rigging my flat so I wouldn't be found out. I studied every piece of literature I could to keep my secret under control. I couldn't lose my job, or I'd lose my chance to track down the one who infected me. I'd lose my revenge."

Korban listened raptly and sipped his beer as Blaze continued. "I found out he had made his way to America, and I took a holiday to follow him here. For a great while he was two steps ahead of me. He knew I was following him and thought he could lose me in the forest up here. Or maybe he had hoped to face off, wolf to wolf. When he vanished I set up camp, bought an old camper for cheap and stocked up the place. I wasn't leaving this forest until I found him and made him pay." He paused again and frowned. "I spent months up here, and lost him. I was about to give up at last and head home to look for fresh leads when I found myself victim to one of the wolf pits.

And the rest, as they say, is history."

Korban mirrored Blaze's frown as he told his tragic tale. "What did he look like, this man— this werewolf you hunted?" A sneaking suspicion began to bubble into Korban's mind.

"He was about your height, built similar to you but a bit thinner and pale-skinned. Red hair, blue eyes. Looked like a pretty harmless fellow, but sadly the worst monsters always do," Blaze said, then curiously asked, "why?"

"I think I know what happened to him." Korban grimaced at the memory. "When I saw Davey's memories I saw how he was turned. I think your red-haired werewolf was caught before you in one of his traps. Davey... he ate him, and became a werewolf."

Blaze stared at Korban for a moment. "You're bloody serious? He..." he trailed off, shook his head and chuckled darkly. "So in the end, Davey was the one who got him. I should thank the wanker." He smirked as Korban gave him a worried glance. "Don't worry; I'm not going to go running back to set him free or anything like that for it. It's just... well, life is strange sometimes, isn't it?"

Korban nodded in agreement. "Amen to that, my friend." He raised an eyebrow as another thought dawned on him. "Do you know how to even find your camp from here?"

"It can't be too difficult to track down. It's an old silver Streamline, a little rough on the outside but the inside is still in pretty decent shape."

It was his turn to raise an eyebrow when Korban choked on his beer. "You all right, Korban?"

"Yeah," Korban chuckled to himself and then lifted his bottle to Blaze's. "Life really is strange."

~*~

Sophie helped the others get things loaded up, but didn't let Korban out of her line of sight. As the others folded tables and chairs and gathered up their belongings, she took down her tent and gathered up the clothes and sleeping bag. Every few moments she glanced up to make sure he was still there, still safe. She watched as he toasted with Blaze, smiled as she heard his laugh. It warmed her heart and filled the hole that was there in his absence.

"You know, it really hurts a guy's feelings when your boyfriend returns and suddenly you're not even giving him the time of day anymore. Even after he was mortally wounded," Freki said, his voice and breathing still a bit strained as his chest healed. "Shame, really, you never told me how ugly he is compared to me."

"Keep it up, Freki, and I'll put a few more holes into you," Sophie teased him back playfully, then added, "I'm glad you're feeling well enough to be yourself again."

"I'm sure a kiss from a fair maiden would help me feel better faster," Freki winked, coughed and winced at the pain as it flared up.

"I'm sure it would," Sophie smirked, and then chastised him. "You really should be resting."

"You know me, I'm not one for following orders," Freki said coolly, but winced and delicately touched his side. "It hurts no matter what I do right now, so I figured at least out here I'd have the pleasure of your company for a little longer anyway."

"You really scared us back there, you know. The way you acted when you got shot, I thought... we all thought you were going to die," Sophie said with a worried frown. "I'm so glad it wasn't silver."

"Me too," Freki grimaced. "It hurt so much, and it still hurts. I can't even imagine what it would be like if that bullet had been made of silver. But we got Hati back, and we rescued Korban and the others from the evil villain. I guess that makes us real, live heroes.

Too bad it seems like my princess is in another castle."

Sophie only smiled and shook her head at him. "You're hopeless, Freki," she said, then went over and gave him a gentle hug. "When you do find the right girl, I know she's going to be lucky to have a guy like you."

He smiled at that. "I'm going to miss you when you're gone."

"I'll miss you too," she said, her expression sobered a bit. "I'm short a best friend after my sister tried to kill me more than once. Perhaps if you and I stay in touch, you'd be up for the challenge?"

Freki grinned. "It would be an honor to be your best friend."

She brightened up and held up her pinky to him. "Pinky promise you'll stay in touch then?"

He curved his pinky to hers and winked again. "Pinky promise."

Val stepped out of the RV and headed over to them. "We're almost ready to hit the road. Before we do, mind if I have a minute alone with Sophie?"

"Sure, no problem. Someone much smarter than me said I should be... ow... resting, ahh, anyway. Which I will, after I go check on one thing." Freki limped stiffly over toward Geri who was loading up the trailer. "Talk to you more while we're on the road Sophie."

Val was quiet for a moment. Sophie followed the female werewolf's gaze as it roamed over the campsite. Her yellow eyes were filled with warmth and adoration as she watched her pack together.

Odin and Geri were fueling up their motorcycles with red gas cans. Skoll was actually smiling, joking with Hati and Steven as they finished loading up one of the compartments alongside the camper. Korban and Blaze stomped out and buried the dying embers of their last campfire. They still had the road ahead, but there was something final about the scene before them. The happy end of a long, painful, and stressful chapter of their lives.

"I don't suppose we can talk you and Korban to making tracks with us? The open road isn't so bad, especially with good company around," Val said, glancing to her.

Sophie smiled and shook her head. "It's tempting, believe me, but we've been away from home long enough."

"Well, shoot. Here I was hoping I wouldn't have to say goodbye," Val sucked in a deep breath, then let it go with a heavy sigh. "I hate goodbyes."

"Me too," Sophie said.

"It's been nice to have another woman around. One that isn't a seventeen-and-a-half-year-old know-it-all." Sophie and Val chuckled.

They stood there and watched the men at work for another quiet moment when Val motioned for her to follow. "Come with me. You're not leaving us, after all you did, without a souvenir."

Perplexed but curious, Sophie trailed after her as Val went into the RV. Inside Evie, Haley, and Connor were up, much to her surprise, and sat waiting at the kitchen table. The three children all had wide, excited grins and scandalously snickered together. Val stood near her kids as she spoke, "Before we were infected, we rode back and forth across the country as our own little club. What started as a hobby among friends became so much more. We became a pack, but before that we were family."

She paused for a moment, this time for dramatic effect, and then nodded to Evie, who giggled in excitement and held up a leather jacket that she'd hidden under the table in her lap.

Sophie's jaw dropped open in surprise as she handed it to her. It was a beautiful, black leather jacket, soft to the touch. Embroidered on the back was the same wolf skull insignia framed by the Valhalla Knights text. "This is for me?" She glanced to each of them in wonder as she held it up.

Val nodded. "You helped bring our family back together. You've more than earned your place in our pack, Sophie. And if you do happen to change your mind, and come ride with us someday, well… I'm sure we can think up a Norse nickname for you too." She gave a playful wink as Sophie beamed. "Well, I guess it's time to round up the men and make tracks. The sooner we put this place behind us, the better I'll feel." She looked to her children. "Now the three of you get on back to bed. Evie, I'm going to let you drive tomorrow so don't be up all night on your phone."

"Okay Mom." Evie stopped to hug Sophie on the way back to her bunk, then murmured excitedly, "I can't wait to be back in range of a decent connection!"

Haley and Connor both hugged her as well, then kissed their mother good night and headed to bed. Val ruffled their blond hair and said, "I'll be right in there to tuck y'all in." She turned to Sophie now that they were alone and caught the longing look in her eyes. "You'll be okay. Just remember that before you became a werewolf, you were a mother. Trust your instincts, and trust yourself. Your wolf will know what you know in your heart to be true. Your son will never, ever be in any danger from your wolf."

Sophie's eyes filled with tears and she clutched the leather jacket to her chest. "Thank you, Valkyrie."

Val went over and gave her a tight hug, then patted her on the shoulder and raised an eyebrow. "This particular jacket was originally meant for Evie when she was old enough, but she agreed that we can get another one made for her when the time comes. You've more than earned your cut these past few days." Then she added excitedly, "Well, what are you waiting for? Try it on! Let's see how it fits."

Sophie pulled on the leather jacket and ran her fingers over the smooth, black leather sleeves. She smiled as it dawned on her that this jacket was hers, the first piece of clothing she had worn in a long while that truly belonged to her. It was a little big and loose on her in some areas, but she wouldn't have it any other way. "It's perfect."

20: HOMEWARD BOUND

Sophie stepped outside in her new leather jacket and was greeted by the rest of the pack and an exuberant round of applause, punctuated by a couple appreciative howls and whistles from Freki and Korban. She smiled brightly at her gathered friends and gave a playful bow. Freki gave her a thumbs up and Korban walked over to her, wrapping his arms around her. "Leather looks good on you," he said, then mischievously grinned and wiggled his eyebrows suggestively.

She slid her arms around him, her fingers played along the back of his neck, and his golden eyes brightened as she moved in close. "I love you." Every word made her feel lighter and happier than before. "Ready to go back?"

He tensed a little but relief filled his eyes and he nodded. "Yeah. Now more than ever. I think I've had my fill of fresh air and wide open spaces." He chuckled darkly then shook his head. "Not really as recently, but you know what I mean."

"Making jokes about it already. Isn't it a bit too soon?" She hugged him tightly, buried her face into his neck, and pressed a kiss along his scar. "We've made it. We're actually going home."

"I can't wait," he said, then squeezed her back before they moved back into the RV as the engines started, and soon they were on the move.

~*~

Blaze ended up changing his mind and joined them on the road after all. His only request was to make a quick errand so he could get his passport and a few personal belongings that he'd stashed away. It didn't take him long to retrieve what he needed and they soon were driving down a long, winding dirt road. As the RV brushed past long branches and grown in grass they all remained on high alert. Everyone breathed a lot easier once the bumpy dirt gave way to smooth asphalt and they were on solid road at last.

Sophie sat next to Korban on the kitchen bench and rested her head on his shoulder as they rode along. He kept his arm around her and let his own chin rest on the top of her head. Steven had opted to go sleep in the master bed in the back while Val and Odin took the helm and drove. The rumble of the engine was echoed by Geri's pickup that followed with most of their bikes, and the louder purr of two motorcycles, ridden by Hati and Skoll. As exhausted as he was, Hati seemed eager to ride with his brother again. Freki had sat across from them in the RV for a while, until the bumps along the road became too much and he finally went into the back to lay down in one of the empty bunks. His soft snoring reverberated along with the engines. Every now and again Sophie would find herself taking a head count, just to make sure the gang was all there. She was pretty certain that she wasn't the only one guilty of this, because every now and then she found Val glancing over her shoulder as she checked on them too.

They were quiet for a long time as they sat together. Blaze dozed off as he leaned back against the booth corner. As tired as they were, neither Korban nor Sophie could sleep. She felt Korban tremble every once in a while and held him tighter. They had freed him and the other men from this nightmare, but it would take some time before they would truly feel safe again. The few minutes she had spent with that sociopath Davey still made her skin crawl. She couldn't even begin to fathom what they'd gone through, trapped all that time in a true monster's lair.

When he trembled again, Sophie lifted her head to meet his gaze. Those warm amber eyes were filled with worry. "What's wrong?" she asked him gently, rubbing his back with her hand.

He calmed under her touch and took in a shuddering breath. "I should be thinking about what happens when we get back, but I keep going back to what happened back there. Not just with Davey but with me. What I did."

Her brow wrinkled in confusion. "What you did?"

"I mean, the way I could influence the others to do things, and not just that," he gazed down at the table. "I was able to see things, when I stared into their eyes. I saw... I saw horrible memories from Davey's past, like some strange... out of body experience. Like I was there reliving everything he experienced, even the smells, the... feelings he had, as twisted as they were." He paused a moment and seemed to inwardly steady himself before he continued, "I could see Spike, er, Steven's memories too, but those were more like watching a home movie or some kind of documentary. I learned a lot about him— saw how he was a good guy in the wrong place at the wrong time. Like Blaze, Hati, and me."

Sophie listened and continued to gently rub small circles along his tense back muscles.

He took another deep breath and relaxed, pressed back into her touch. "I keep thinking about it, and it scares me. Almost more than anything else that has happened."

"What about it scares you, love?" she softly asked.

He thought about it for a moment, and then lifted his gaze to hers once more. "I'm afraid of having power over someone else. No one should be forced to do something against their own free will. That kind of power... it shouldn't exist. I'm scared because Davey had the same power too. I don't want to end up like him. I know I'm not a cannibal with some whacked out fantasy fight club, but I'm terrified that I'll lose control of my power, or maybe I've accidentally used it before, or somehow, maybe, worst of all... I've used it on you."

Sophie gave him a serious look and leaned in, pressed her soft lips to the rough stubble that had grown in along his chin. "My love, you will never, ever be anything remotely close to that monster."

She cupped his cheek with the palm of her hand and swiped a tear away with the pad of her thumb as it trailed down. "The fact that you are so worried about everyone else when you've just discovered this incredible ability that you have... it's just one of the many reasons why I love you. And one of the many reasons why I know you'd never abuse your power like Davey did." She smiled to him. "And you should know me well enough by now to know I don't do anything that I don't want to do. I love you, Korban. I love you. That isn't your power influencing me. It never has been. That night when we first made love, you told me you loved me, remember?"

He nodded, his lower lip trembled and she leaned in, capturing it in a kiss. Her arms wrapped around him again and she held him close even when she parted from their sweet kiss. "I'm sorry I couldn't say those words back to you that night. I wasn't ready because a lot of people I loved had broken my heart. I never doubted the truth in your words. I just thought that I would have more time to say it back. My head got in the way of my heart then, but I won't waste my chance to say it to you now, or ever again. I love you. I love you, Korban." Her lips hungrily pressed to his. He returned her kiss, and for a few blissful moments they were lost in each other.

When she pulled away he smiled, all the worries seemed to vanish from her reassuring words and kisses. "I love you so much. I don't know how you do it. How do you always seem to know exactly what to say to make me feel better?"

"It's my special power." Sophie ran her fingers through his hair as she winked.

He chuckled lightly and pulled her in close again. Their lips met, and they lost several more wonderful minutes together.

~*~

It was a little after three in the morning when their caravan pulled up to the garage. Korban practically had his face pressed against the window as he repeatedly read the sign. Cyrus Autos was still where they'd left her, though she had her own set of scars now too. Metal rigging was wrapped around the garage for support, and bright orange and yellow signs cautioned that the site was under construction. A huge plastic tarp covered one of the car port entrances. For a moment Korban wondered if RJ and Alex were even able to stay there while it was being repaired, but then a light clicked on in one of the upstairs windows and his heart sang. They were home!

Sophie was saying her good-byes to the others, exchanging phone numbers and hugs. Korban politely said his good byes but found himself alone with Hati and Blaze. Steven had said his good byes long before, and they agreed not to interrupt his sleep. Hati gave him a hug and murmured a quick farewell, then hurried back to his bike, as though he didn't want anyone see him cry. "See you around, my friend," Korban said with a smile and watched him head back to his bike, leaving him alone yet again with Blaze.

"I'm not sure I can ever repay you for all you did for me, for freeing us all from that hell, and helping me put my case to rest. If you should ever find yourself across the pond, know you're always welcome. The world can be a dark and scary place, but at least we've got mates to light the way, yeah?" He pulled a business card from his pocket and slipped it into Korban's hand as he gave him a firm handshake. "That's my personal number; I don't give that out very often. If you should ever need help, know you've got an ally in me. It's nice to know that not all Yankee werewolves are barmy lunatics."

Korban only grinned and chuckled. "Wow, did I hear right? Was that a joke? There's hope for you yet, Blaze," he paused and read the business card and corrected himself, "rather, Nigel… 'Blazer'?"

"It's Blazier, but Blaze is just fine, Lobo." Blaze smirked to him, and then clapped him on the shoulder. "Cheers, mate."

"Cheers." Korban nodded back, then watched as he headed back into the RV.

Sophie walked over beside him and they waved as the caravan pulled away and drove off into the night, towards the airport to drop off Blaze, who was taking the next flight out, and then to the open road. Sophie slid her hand into his, and as their friends rounded the corner and headed out of sight, she turned to look up at the sign. "I've missed this place so much," she said.

"Me too." Korban felt anxious to see his two best friends – his brothers – again.

They walked around the corner and found the side entrance repaired, and a new door in place of the old one. The area smelled of fresh paint, wood, plaster, and faintly of lingering smoke and burnt oil. They followed the cleared path through the garage to the steps on the inside. There were still some scorch marks along some areas and it was littered with piles of plywood, sheets of plastic, and paint buckets. But no matter what, it was home.

They reached the inside door to the apartment, and before

Korban could knock, the door opened and Alex greeted them. He blinked in disbelief for a moment, rubbed his sleepy eyes, and then his face erupted into a huge grin. "Korban? Sophie? It's really you?"

Korban felt a lump form in his throat. There were moments not that long ago that he worried he would never see Alex again. And now he stood there, his arm still in a sling, but that same bright smile returning in full force. Like his patched-up garage, he would be okay. Korban swallowed the emotional lump down and cracked, "You expecting someone else at this hour? The garage must be doing pretty well if you can afford a call girl."

Alex laughed, then wrapped his good arm around him in fierce hug, before he let him go to do the same to Sophie. As he moved in to hug her, he realized what he was about to do and stopped himself. Sophie only smiled to him. "It's fine now, Alex," she said, and insisted on wrapping him into a hug. "I've missed you too."

Elated, Alex cheered into the apartment, "RJ! Lobo's back! Sophie and Lobo are home!"

A surprised, *"What?!"* came from the back bedroom, followed by some bumps and thumps, and then RJ came racing out in his pajama bottoms, still tying his robe around him as he rushed up the hall. His face brightened as Alex stepped aside and ushered them in. "Dammit, Korban!" RJ had tears in his eyes and he wrapped him into a powerful but welcoming hug. "You had us both scared! Where the hell have you two been?"

"That's a really, really long and complicated story," Korban said, gripping RJ tightly and fighting back tears of his own. "Think we can put on some coffee first?"

RJ nodded, holding him for another moment before he glanced to Sophie who nodded, and he put an arm around her too. "I'm so glad you're both all right. And human again too! The last we heard,

Sergeant McKinnon was looking everywhere for you two as Wolven." He hesitated a moment, the unspoken worry returned to his eyes and his expression sobered. "We're supposed to report in the moment we hear anything from you two, but... to hell with it. We'll go to the station tomorrow after you've rested. You both look like you could use a hot meal and a shower. No offense."

Korban chuckled and shook his head. "None taken. A shower sounds pretty damn good right about now."

RJ soon had a pot of coffee brewing and a pan of bacon and eggs sizzling on the stove, and they gathered around the kitchen table. When Sophie put her hand in Korban's and squeezed it, he was certain that this was his own slice of heaven. "I'm glad you two are here," Korban said. "I was afraid that... because we ran off, that they'd throw you in jail because of me."

RJ flipped the eggs and bacon using only the skillet and then turned his head in his direction with a grim smile. "Oh, believe me, they wanted to. Sergeant McKinnon actually stood up for me as a character witness, but it was my principal who saved me in the end. Talked them out of taking away one of his best teachers right before finals. Commissioner DeRusso ended up agreeing to let me out on house arrest. At least I scored a neat new accessory for all the trouble." He lifted his pant leg and revealed a shiny, black ankle monitor that had a slow blinking light on it.

Korban and Sophie exchanged a glance, looking guilty, but he shrugged and smirked. "Hey, what can I say? If anything it's helped me through the end of the school year. Gave me a little street cred and impressed some of my tough guys. Now that they think I'm a real gangster they've been behaving more in my class." He then added pointedly after a pause, "It's okay. I'm fine. Believe me. Especially now that we know you're both safe, sound, and home again."

He plated up their late night snack – more like an early breakfast at this hour – and served them all steaming mugs of coffee with extra cream and sugar. After they got a few bites down, RJ reluctantly asked, "Where were you guys? Most of Syracuse was on the lookout for you. The news alerted everyone that two Wolven were on the loose. They even had a press conference and everything. Not to mention the reward that your husband posted."

"Lucas offered a reward?" Sophie sounded surprised at first, then frowned anxiously at the news.

"Yeah, and let's say the payout is better than the lottery at this point. I could open a whole chain of garages with that kind of bank. Not that I would sell you guys out, or anything." Alex blushed and looked a bit sheepish.

"You'll have to forgive him, he hasn't been sleeping well between his arm healing, his refusal to take his pain killers, and worrying about you two." RJ sipped his coffee and sighed. "Screw it. It's late. You two look like you've been through hell, and as much as I am dying to know where you've been, and what happened, I think it's better you get some rest. We'll have all tomorrow at the station to go over the whole story anyway."

"Thank you, RJ, for understanding," Sophie said with a small smile. Her mind was still reeling at their revelation about Lucas, but her brain was just too tired to process it just yet.

They finished their meals, then RJ gathered their plates up so they could go shower. Though she had showered a lot more recently than Korban, Sophie joined him and after they helped wash one another, they held each other for a few minutes as hot water streamed down from above. His absence was still too fresh, and it would take time for her to let him out of her sight if she could help it. Korban felt much fresher after a long needed shower, coffee back in his system, and Alex's robe around him. He let Sophie borrow his own and they headed for his bedroom. It wasn't too different from how he'd left it, and he realized that the upstairs apartment seemed to thankfully be in better shape than the garage below. Korban was all too happy to crawl into bed with Sophie, and as they held one another it didn't take long for both of them to finally drift off to a truly restful sleep.

~*~

When they awoke it was the afternoon and a new anxiety began to take root as they got dressed and prepared to report in to the police station. Sergeant McKinnon hadn't steered them wrong yet, Korban tried to reassure her, but Sophie had a sinking feeling in her stomach that she couldn't shake. She caught a glimpse of his furrowed brow while he shaved and knew he was just as worried as she was about what would happen next. She brushed her teeth with her toothbrush, one of the few precious possessions that she could call her own, and reflected on what they'd gone through. He was carefully patting down his face with aftershave when she finished brushing and turned to him. "No matter what happens, from here on out, it's you and me. We've faced impossible situations before. We'll get through this together," she said, and gave him a hopeful smile, leaning in, kissing his now smooth cheek.

Together, they dressed; Korban in his nicest interview outfit, a sharp, charcoal gray suit that seemed to hang a little loosely on his frame. Sophie held back a growl when her thoughts briefly went to Davey, and hoped he was feeling hungry at that very moment. She didn't let herself linger on it for long, there were more important matters at hand and that monster had robbed enough time from her and Korban. Alex had dug up a plain but nice black dress and pair of matching flats that had belonged to his mother from up in the attic. They fit decently enough and she thanked him. "When we get back, the first thing I plan on doing is taking you clothes shopping," Korban vowed.

Together, they headed to the car and sat in the back. RJ drove while Alex rode shotgun. The car ride was a quiet but tense one. Sophie held Korban's hand to keep herself from trembling, and her touch calmed him as much as his did for her.

Together they walked into the bustling police station. Most people were too busy dealing with their own problems at hand to spare them a second glance. However a few more observant witnesses did stare and whispered in wonder as Sophie walked past. She swore she saw someone snap a quick picture on their cell phone, but a candid paparazzi photo was the least of her concerns at the moment.

When they went to sign in with Patty she greeted them with a warm smile, until she realized it was them, and her eyes went round and she gave an excited little bounce. "Oh! The Sarge will be so happy you're back!" She cheered, then ushered them to his office. She knocked raptly on the door and peered in ahead of them. "Sergeant McKinnon, RJ Ramirez is here and he's brought Korban Diego and Sophie Bane here to see you. Oh, and Alex too."

"What?! Get in here, all of you!" He stood up at his desk, then asked Patty, "Can you get Andy for me, Patty? I think he should be here for this."

"Of course, Sergeant," Patty headed off to find his partner.

They filed in and sat down. Tim watched them with a neutral expression in his piercing blue eyes as he closed the door and went behind his desk. He hadn't changed much in the time they had been gone, though the dark circles under his eyes seemed darker, and his neatly trimmed beard was a little longer than usual. "The whole city's been in a tizzy looking for you two. I can't even begin to tell you how many man hours have been put into tracking you both down. Not even including the hundreds of calls trying to cash in on supposed leads. They've been searching for you by land, by water, and by air.

The damn press is breathing down my neck every day. It's been one hot mess after another." He paced behind his desk as he talked, then stopped, turned to them. "Still, I'm glad you're both back and human again. Well, human-ish I suppose."

The office door opened again and Sergeant Ellyk stepped in. The tall, lanky black man broke into a wide grin at the sight of them. His hair was a little unkempt, and there was a sprinkle of salt in his short, dark curls. "Wow, we thought for sure we'd be finding you with a lot more fur on ya. Welcome back."

"Thank you," Sophie said as Andy closed the door again and stood over behind Tim's desk. "It really is good to be back."

"All right, before we get the details on where you have been and what you remember, I'll give you the rundown," Tim said, then sat in his chair and pulled out a camera on a small tripod. "I'm going to be recording this, because no doubt this is going to blow up in a big way. Er, sorry Alex, bad choice of wording."

Alex only shrugged and smiled. It was a rare sight to see him so quiet but the tension was definitely as pungent as the tiny pine trees that perfumed the air. Tim continued on as a little red light began to glow on the camera and he pointed it to where Korban and Sophie sat across from him. "All right, here we go. Sergeant Tim McKinnon here with Sergeant Andrew Ellyk, interviewing Korban Diego and Sophie Bane. Witnessed by Ramiel Ramirez, Mr. Diego's legal sponsor, and Alejandro Cyrus." He rattled off the date, time, and the case number, and then asked, "So, what do you remember from the time you have been missing?"

Korban drew in a shaky breath. Sophie took his hand as he began their horrific tale. He did most of the talking at first, telling the story from his perspective. He started from the time he could remember them waking naked in the forest, and continued on, only leaving out some of the more intimate details. When he described being captured and tortured by Davey the color drained from everyone's faces as he went into painful detail. Sophie didn't realize just how bad it had been for him, and only regretted not punching Davey even harder. She squeezed his hand when he got choked up during certain details. There wasn't much he left out, but he was careful to stick to nicknames, except for when it came to David Bailey and his two henchmen. The room was silent when he finished.

Finally, Tim cleared his throat. "And you, Mrs. Bane? Where were you during most of… all this?"

She told her side of things, a much more pleasant side of the story. She was thankful that Val's pack used nicknames, and was careful to use them like Korban did to protect the ones who mattered. When she had completed her story, the room went quiet again.

"Do you think you can describe how to get to this barn, so we can send authorities in to arrest David Bailey and his pals?" Andy asked softly.

Korban nodded. "Yes. He is extremely dangerous and even though we left him in a cage, do not underestimate what he is capable of. He should be kept away from other werewolves especially since he can control them."

Andy nodded, rubbed his chin thoughtfully, and looked to his partner. "Thank you, Mr. Diego." Tim had a grim look on his face as he reached over and shut off the camcorder, then continued, "You're sure it's true, what you said about the whole… monster mojo? You were able to calm those other wolves down and… control them?"

Korban bobbed his head again in affirmation and looked worried. "I don't understand how or why, exactly. The only thing we had in common really was that our eyes stay yellow. I don't want to use that power again if I can help it. I wouldn't want to force anyone to do something they wouldn't want to do."

"Still, you helped those wolves calm down with your ability, that's not something that should go to waste. Think of the lives you could save if you could just talk someone down from going rabid," Tim said while scratching his goatee. "You've always been special, Korban. This just adds another element to it."

The door burst open and Commissioner DeRusso strode in, accompanied by several officers. Tim straightened up and frowned. "What's the meaning of this, Commissioner? I'm in the middle of an interview with Mr. Diego and Mrs. Bane."

"While I appreciate your help in locating our missing lycanthropes, I'm afraid I have to intervene at this time," she began as the officers moved behind Sophie and Korban, and before they could move two familiar sounding clicks sounded, and they both cried out in surprised pain as tranquilizers struck them.

"What the…? Why?" Korban fearfully stammered as his vision began to swim and his limbs went numb.

The officer behind him snapped silver cuffs around his wrists, which itched and burned only a little as the tranquilizer took hold. "What did they do wrong? They turned themselves in!" RJ demanded angrily, but the Commissioner stood her ground as silver cuffs were snapped around Sophie's wrists as well.

"Mr. Ramirez, thank you for doing your duty as a sponsor and upstanding citizen. However at this time we've deemed these two werewolves extremely dangerous and unpredictable. Until we know more about that serum that they were exposed to before they vanished, I'm afraid we have to take them in. I'm suspending your role as Mr. Diego's legal sponsor, and you'll be free to go. We'll get that monitor off your ankle and you can resume your life as normal."

"Wait! No!" RJ protested. "Please, Commissioner, they're

cooperating. They haven't done anything wrong!"

"It's not about what they haven't done, at least not yet. We have a lot to learn from that serum, and I'm not putting my city at risk again of some new super infection by letting them roam free," DeRusso snapped sharply. "Until we know what it is we're up against, we have no choice but to hold them in quarantine."

Korban's eyes went round and he moaned weakly, "No..."

Sophie struggled against her bindings as the officers heaved her up to her feet, half leading and half dragging her toward the door. Two other officers guided Korban along the way. "Please, don't do this! We've been fine since we turned back!" Sophie pleaded as the room began to sway and warp around them.

"I'm sorry Mrs. Bane, but we don't have a choice in this matter. I have to do what's best for Syracuse." DeRusso's tone went cold as she followed them out of Tim's office despite the protests and discontent coming from all their friends in the room.

Together they were escorted towards the van that waited outside, and together they were escorted to the facility at Hutchings. Korban's eyes were half-glazed over by the time they arrived. "Korban," Sophie murmured to him weakly, struggling to stay conscious as they opened the van doors. "I love you."

"Sophie..." he whispered softly back, "Love you..."

Together they were dragged into the complex, past doctors in white lab coats and nurses in a rainbow of scrubs. They moved through heavy, alarmed and armored doors though a hall that reeked of antiseptic and anxiety. Sophie's stomach twisted and churned and her heart raced.

The officers stopped to open a door in this hall, and to Sophie's horror, the other men continued dragging Korban past her, further down the corridor. "No!" Sophie cried out, her voice hoarse and heavy. "Korban! Please, don't take him from me!"

"Sophie!" Korban's voice came, a panicked but feeble cry as they began to go through another set of doors. He struggled enough to turn back and she saw pure fear in his yellow eyes.

"Korban!" She called back to him, but the tranquilizer was making the white hall twist and spin, or maybe they had lifted her up and around.

The doors that they had taken Korban beyond closed with a resonating and final slam. She still writhed against them, but her body had become too heavy to move. She wanted to scream but the only sound that came from her now was a low, desperate moan.

Alone, she finally succumbed to the darkness, her last fleeting thought was of Korban and their brief, blissful time together.

~*~

~*~

HUNGRY FOR MORE?

Sophie and Korban's adventure is only beginning!

To be continued in *Infected Moonlight*, book three of the

Tainted Moonlight Series!

AVAILABLE NOW

Sink your teeth into a special preview on the next page!

~*~

Sophie's head throbbed as she stirred and woke from a deep, troubled sleep. She didn't feel rested but instead somehow more drained of energy, as though she hadn't slept at all. The memories of horrible dreams still flashed in her mind until she remembered that the nightmare was real.

Her eyes slowly opened and came to focus on an unfamiliar ceiling. White panels and a pair of long, fluorescent lights were fixed above her. The room had the same stinging, antiseptic smell of most hospital rooms. She went to move her hand to rub her aching forehead but restraints bound her wrists and ankles to the sides of the bed. She lifted her hand as far as it would go and saw silver chains carefully weaved around the bindings. It wasn't burning her, but it strengthened the straps.

She winced as her pulse seemed to echo the ache in her skull, and looked around the room. It was clean and fairly empty, with only her hospital bed and a small, long table and chair that was pushed over against the wall nearby. High, narrow windows lined the one wall and let sunlight stream in through the frosted panels.

Her mouth felt dry and she made a face as she tried to speak in a hoarse voice. "Help," she said, clearing her throat as best as she could and fought back the wave of nausea coming over her. A little louder, she managed to roughly yelp out, "Help!"

The door opened like magic, and a nurse stepped in, a surgeon's mask over her nose and mouth and a plastic clipboard in her hands. She peered at Sophie over a pair of safety glasses. The rest of her was covered in long scrubs. "Oh, Mrs. Bane, you're awake. Good."

She scribbled down something and Sophie grimaced, clenched her hands, and stretched them. She sat up as best as she could so she could put herself in a better position, and asked in a gravelly whisper, "Where's Korban?"

The nurse gave her a quizzical look, and then came a flash of recognition. "Oh, Mr. Diego. He's secured in his room. Don't worry; he won't bother you in here." Sophie slowly shook her head, about to protest that he'd saved her life, and wouldn't be a bother at all, when the nurse smiled brightly and continued on, "Besides you have a very special visitor who's been waiting quite a while for you to wake up."

"Visitor?" Sophie hoarsely repeated as the nurse opened the door and ushered her guest in. Her heart skipped a beat as time froze and a chill coursed through her entire body. "Lucas."

~*~

WANT MORE MOONLIGHT NOW?

Visit the official website taintedmoonlight.com for news, updates, character biographies, interviews with the author, and even more bonus content!

Share *Tainted Moonlight* on your social media with friends and help the Pack grow! Like *Tainted Moonlight* on Facebook and follow @AuthorErinKelly on Twitter to participate in full moon giveaways and contests that feature exclusive rewards for Pack Mates.

JOIN THE PACK TODAY!

~*~

SPECIAL MESSAGE TO THE PACK

Thank you again to my dear friends Tina and Lisa for helping me dot my I's and cross my T's and keep all my werewolves in order, and an infinite amount of gratitude to the lovely Erin Al-Mehairi for editing my story. A special thank you again to my parents for your continuous love and support, especially to my Dad for helping to promote and share my book with his coworkers and friends, and to Mom and Bud for helping watch my fur babies while I travel around to do promoting of my own for my series. A special howl out to Uncle Miles for being a great movie buddy and for also encouraging me to keep writing. I'm sure I'll be hearing from you soon and you'll be nipping my heels to get the next book out ASAP (and don't worry, it will be!). Thanks to Fay, Carrie, Tina (again!) and Linda for helping woman my booths during events, you ladies are amazing. Also a very special thank you to Chelsea, Mae, Nina, and The Roost Podcast's league of awesome interns for helping me navigate conventions. Your advice from your show experience has been extremely helpful and I look forward to all of our events together this year (and hopefully many more to come)!

My eternal gratitude to Sohaib with Fictional Frontiers, WebcamNick on YouTube, and Tom Clark and the guys of Necrocasticon for helping promote my series on their platforms. (If you want to check out my interviews with them, I have links posted on taintedmoonlight.com).

Thank you as well to two special "Saints" for their unexpected and welcome support. A special mention to the "Funny Man" himself, David Della Rocco for becoming the first celebrity to purchase a copy of *Tainted Moonlight*. I hope you enjoy the story so far and continue to follow the series! A thank you as well to Sean Patrick Flanery for your advice from one author to another, as well as the social media bump on Twitter when my novel first debuted. Shine until tomorrow my famous friends.

I really can't thank you all enough for your feedback, reviews, love and support. Thank you to all my friends, family, and the growing community of fans. I would be nothing without you my fellow Pack Mates! Until next time everyone, be well!

~ *Erin Kelly*

ABOUT THE AUTHOR

Erin Kelly lives in Syracuse, New York with her precocious Siamese cat Taro, and her dogs Winchester and MacManus. When she is not writing about werewolves, she is often drawing, reading, swimming at the gym, or can be found at several local karaoke bars belting out ballads by the Backstreet Boys with her friends.

Tainted Moonlight is her debut novel and the first in the series, with sequel *Captured Moonlight*, and the third book in the series, *Infected Moonlight*, now available, and more to come soon!